Traveling Money

H. ROGER STEWART

MW01709463

PublishAmerica
Baltimore

First printing

ISBN: 1-60813-494-6
PUBLISHED BY PUBLISHAMERICA, LLLP
www.publishamerica.com
Baltimore

Printed in the United States of America

A Sequel to *Deceived*

In "Deceived," Jack Stevens investigates the death of his brother, John, by a hit and run driver. The local police believe it is an accident, pure and simple. Jack believes otherwise because his brother whispers a name to him just before he dies. Jack starts his investigation and it leads to several suspects, including his brother's old girlfriend, Ralene. Because Jack is successful in solving the death of his brother, he is asked to help in the investigation of a local drug operation. His tendency to bend the rules and his unorthodox methods land Jack on the wrong side of the law. He is offered a get out of jail free card by the local DA. Jack's assignment is to infiltrate a local motorcycle gang. During this undercover assignment, Jack meets two young ladies. One, June, is a newspaper reporter, who helps Jack get information leading to the downfall of the drug operation. The other, Barbara, is a special prosecutor in the Attorney General's Office. After she is killed in a drug raid, Jack realizes, too late, that he loves her. Barbara becomes Jack's guardian angel and provides much needed help to Jack. When he is asked, again, to help in another narcotics investigation,

Jack throws himself into this operation with a vengeance. With the arrest of several major drug kingpins, Jack heads back to his home town. He leaves the newspaper reporter standing on the curb in front of the newspaper office. She has a story to write and Jack has to remain anonymous. As he rides off into the night, little did he know what awaits him.

Part 1

The Killer

He was born August 30, 1920 in a hospital in Ashland, Kentucky. He was a premature baby weighing 4 pounds and 3 ounces and he fought for his life from the moment of his birth. The Nurses and Doctors were amazed at the size of the child's hands. They looked as though they belong on a child a couple of years old. His Father was not around because he was killed in a vehicle accident six months earlier. His Mother would have her hands full raising him by herself. She would devote her entire life to him.

His first six weeks of life were spent in an incubator, an oxygen tube up his little nose. Needles, piercing his tiny arms, kept life saving fluids dripping into his body. The Doctors were amazed at his will to survive. He fought off high temperature and infection for several weeks. Amazingly, in those weeks he was able to gain weight. By the time he was six weeks old, he had gained two pounds.

It was the happiest day of his mother's life when she was able to bring him home. He was still very small, but even she could sense his desire to live. Mom doted on him every day. She was lucky that her husband had been heavily insured and the insurance money would allow her to stay home for many years to raise her child. She was not extravagant and managed her money very well. His first four years were spent in the company of his Mother. He was never away from her, not even for a minute. The only way his grandparents could see him was to come to him. Even then, his Mother was always around.

At the age of four, she started him on piano and dancing lessons. She did not allow him to have a normal childhood, no friends or playmates. By the time he entered first grade, he was the target of school yard bullies. His answer was always, run home to Mama. While grade school was almost unbearable to him, he did manage to get excellent grades. Because he was a smart child and very small, the time spent between school and home was his worst fear. That's when the teachers could not protect him.

Even in grade school, he had violent thoughts about his tormenters and he spent many hours thinking of revenge. High school, for him, was many times worse than he had ever imagined. With only one high school in town, he was thrown in with the many different classes of society. He knew being the smallest child; he would never be able to play sports so he chose to be the smartest kid in all of his classes. Four years of being the butt of jokes, because of his size, festered inside him. It grew until it became an obsession. Some day he would make all the pretty people sorry for the way they treated him. In fact, he considered most people unworthy to live. He hated high school and begged his Mom to home school him. She applied through the local school board but was not qualified to teach because she did not finish school herself. Her only alternative was to walk him to school and be there when school let out. His tormentors were unrelenting in their harassment.

He graduated first in his class, number 1 out of 153. During the summer of 1940, he worked at the same hospital he was born in. As an orderly for the hospital, he came in contact with many people. That summer, he decided he wanted to work in the medical profession. He would get the respect he craved. His Mother died in 1946. He was 26 at the time and had just moved out of his Mother's house. He needed privacy for what he planned. Some people said she died of a broken heart and other rumors said he killed her. Her death was never questioned and the county authorities never pursued the cause. In his twisted mind, he blamed the pretty people for his Mother's death and swore vengeance on all of them.

Thirty years old and he still carried the festering sores from his past. All the pretty people still bothered him and he felt a deep hatred for them. He felt it was his duty to rid the world of the unworthy. Everyone that had been cruel to him, when he was young, was scattered to the four corners of the earth. While he may not be able to find the specific tormentors, there would be many who would take their place and sate his desires. He was a time bomb just waiting to explode on an unsuspecting world. tick...tick...tick...tick...

Part 2

The Victims

February, 1962

He stood in the shadows as Emily Watson walked from the hospital to her car in the parking lot. Several of the security lights were out and she was unaware of his presence. His blood was coursing through his veins and his heart was beating rapidly. Even though it was late February, sweat trickled down his back and drops of perspiration beaded on his face. "I'll show everybody," he muttered, "The unworthy will fear me."

He had been small all of his young life. He was tired of being picked on and in his late teens and early adulthood, he worked out every day. He didn't want the body of a muscle man; he wanted powerful arms and hands. He had waited for this night for many years. Even as a teenager, he would say to himself, someday, they all will pay the price. That day had arrived and Emily would be his first victim.

Just as Emily's hand touched the door handle of her car, he stepped up behind her and grabbed her by the throat. Slipping a rope around her neck, he forced her into the car, making her slide across the bench seat of the old

Chevrolet. "Get down in the floor," he yelled, as he threw her purse and a seat cushion at her. Emily was barely 5' tall and had to use the seat cushion to see over the hood of the car.

He was so excited he could hardly drive the car out of the parking lot. Emily offered him the few dollars she had in her purse, but he told her, "Shut up, I don't want your money."

Emily asked, "What do you want? Are you going to rape me?"

"No," he replied, as he jerked on the rope. "Just be quiet."

Emily felt the car go over a railroad track. The only railroad track she knew of was southwest of town. As he continued to drive, Emily became more and more frightened. The dashboard lights illuminated drool as it rolled down his chin. With a swipe of his left sleeve, he caught it before if fell on his shirt.

He kept thinking, I can do this, I know I can. About twenty minutes elapsed before he stopped the car, jerked the rope tight and pulled Emily up in the seat beside him. As she turned to look at him, she recognized him.

"My God, it's you. Why are you doing this? I've known you since I was a young girl. Why are you doing this?"

"Because I can," he replied. With that statement, he reached over and wrapped his hands around her throat. Emily struggled violently, but she was no match for the power in those hands. Soon, she was not breathing. Emily became the first victim of many to come.

Starting Emily's car, he drove twenty minutes to the abandoned family farm. There, he removed the sod and dug a hole several feet deep. Just before placing Emily's body in the cold earth, he removed one of her earrings. After placing her in the ground, he reached down and placed a nickel on each of her eyes. After the body was covered, he replaced the sod and started looking around for a spot for his next victim.

Driving back towards town, he parked Emily's car in some underbrush and proceeded to wipe all traces of his finger prints from the car. The steering wheel, the gear shift lever, and the door handles were all methodically wiped clean. Even Emily's purse was given the once over, just in case. Walking a few hundred yards down the road, he took off into the woods. Back in his apartment, by 5:30 AM, he anxiously awaited for the sun to rise on a new day. He was already thinking about a new victim.

Jim Stone was sitting on the banks of the Big Sandy River about a mile east of the oil refinery. Jim liked to fish at night and he had sat there many times before, a kerosene lantern lighting his little area of the river bank. Jim was a bachelor and answered to no one. He could fish all night if he wanted to and many times he did just that. Before Jim left home, he packed a few sandwiches and had planned to spend most of the night on the river bank. He had already caught two big catfish and wanted a couple more before he headed back home. He would never accomplish that goal.

The strangler was highly agitated that night. He was out trolling for his next victim and when he drove past the refinery, he noticed Jim's car parked along the railroad tracks. His breathing rate increased and his heart pounded in his chest. He parked his car in a little turn out about fifty feet past Jim's car. He climbed the little bank to the rail road tracks and started walking west towards Jim's private little world. The refinery road was heavily traveled west of the refinery. To the east, you were lucky if you saw a car all night. The strangler had chosen his next victim and the perfect place to escape prying eyes.

When he was opposite Jim's car, he quietly slipped down to the foot path to the river bank. The water was low because of a lack of rain upstream and a ten foot swath of sand and mud made it easy to see Jim's lantern. He could walk within twenty feet of Jim and still be in total darkness. He inched closer and closer as Jim was taking a big catfish off his line. The strangler's voice boomed out, "How are you doing, looks like you caught a big one."

Jim dropped the fish and spun around in the direction of the voice.

"Man, you scared the hell out of me. You shouldn't be sneaking up on people like that. You could get shot."

As he inched closer, he kept repeating over and over in his mind, I can do this again, I know I can.

He told Jim, "Don't talk to me that way; you don't own the river bank."

Jim was angry and spoke up, "Who the hell are you and what are you doing skulking around at 10:30 at night?"

The strangler muttered, "I will do this," and exploded towards Jim. Jim put his hands up to protect himself, but it was already too late. Huge, powerful hands were already wrapped around his throat. The hands were crushing his wind pipe and Jim was helpless to prevent it. As his vision faded, his arms dropped limply at his side. Jim became victim #2.

He carried Jim's body up the foot path and dumped the body in the trunk of his car. After driving for forty five minutes, he pulled into the same abandoned farm. The same as before, he dug a grave. Going through Jim's pockets, he found a fountain pen, which he kept as a reminder of the occasion. Throwing the body in the grave, he reached down and placed a nickel on each eye. He was beside himself with excitement and he spoke aloud, "That's twice and nobody is the wiser." Later, he sat in his apartment, relishing every moment of both murders. He knew he could do it again. It was so easy. All those years of abuse was boiling inside him just like a dam ready to burst, spilling its destructive force down stream. He was ready to kill again. One month later, he spotted his next victim, Jane Ulster.

Jane was a vulnerable person. The strangler learned of her divorce through the local newspaper and a co-worker informed him about her losing her job at the real estate office. His day job kept him busy most of the time, but he could take off a day every now and then to extend the week end. He told his associates he was going hunting and the one thing he failed to mention was that his prey is human. Jane presented a problem because she did not leave the house very often. After a few weeks of observing Jane, he learned that she frequented Wink's, a bar on the outskirts of town. Jane would sit in one of the booths in the back of the bar. Little candles sat on each of the tables to give a romantic air for young couples frequenting Wink's. Jane would always snuff out the candle, as most patrons did, to get a little more privacy in the darkened back of the bar. She would not get falling down drunk, but rather drink just enough to forget her troubles for a few hours.

On a Friday night, in late July, Jane left the house, walking on an exceptionally balmy evening. She didn't drive because she knew she was going to over indulge that night as it was the anniversary of her divorce. After a half hour of walking, she entered Wink's and the place was unusually empty that night. She sat in her regular booth, snuffed out the candle and after three hours and several drinks; Jane was able to forget her troubles. She paid her tab and started walking home. Little did she know he was waiting on her, just a half block down the street? When he saw her come out of the bar, he stepped out of his car into the shadows. Jane didn't see him until it was too late.

He grabbed her, put a piece of tape over her mouth and shoved her violently in the car. He slipped a length of rope around her neck and ordered her to get in the floor and be quiet. She kept trying to scream, but the tape kept her lips closed. His face was barely illuminated by the dash board lights. Jane had no idea who he was or why he was doing this to her. About thirty minutes later, he parked in front of the gate at the farm, pulled Jane up by the rope and wrapped his powerful hands around her neck. As Jane struggled, her last thought was, this will release me from my suffering. Again, he dug the hole and placed her body in the cold earth. And again, after placing her in the ground, he put a nickel on each eye.

Jane's problems were over. That made three murders and he was getting bolder. Jane had been snatched from a city street and no one noticed. The adrenaline rush was what he craved. Just before he covered the body, he removed one of Jane's ear rings. He had a self satisfied look on his face and he realized that while it had been so easy, the last two murders were very close together. He would have to control his urges for a while. He had the rest of his life to rid the world of the unworthy. He contained his urges for nine months. In April of 63, his 4th victim was chosen.

Raymond Strong was up before dawn and out in the woods just before day break. He really wasn't a hunter, but he took a single shot 22 rifle with him. He never knew when he might encounter a squirrel out in the woods and squirrel meat, with all the fixings, made an excellent stew. This morning, he was looking for nuts and berries. Raymond was more a vegetarian than a meat eater, but a little meat every now and then was okay by him. Raymond worked at a local fire department for twenty one years and was getting tired of seeing people die from careless smokers and faulty wiring. He had the option of retiring after twenty years service and recently put those plans into motion. With his pension and a little side job, he could survive quite well.

The strangler was out trolling for his next victim. He was on Cannonsburg Road and drove by as Raymond was getting out of the car. As his headlights illuminated Raymond, his heart started beating faster. He looked in his mirrors and did not see any other lights and drove on for another fifty yards. He pulled off the road and parked his car in a stand of trees. He walked along the tree line back to Raymond's car. As he walked down the path towards Raymond, his heart rate increased rapidly, his breathing was coming in gasps and the sweat beaded on his forehead and upper lip. "I can do this again," he muttered softly.

Around 6:30, Raymond was busy picking berries and did not see or hear the person sneaking up on him. When that person spoke, Raymond was startled and spun around to face the intruder.

"You scared the crap out of me," Raymond said.

"I'm sorry," he replied, "I didn't mean to."

The intruder extended his hand as if to shake hands. Raymond stuck out his right hand and said, "I'm Raymond."

The intruder said, "You unworthy bastard, I'm going to kill you."

With those words barely out of his mouth, he struck Raymond in the head, knocking him to the ground. The intruder was on top of Raymond in a heart beat, hands wrapped around his throat. Dazed from the blow, Raymond started struggling after a few seconds. By then, it was too late. As the intruder's hands crushed Raymond's esophagus, his struggling ceased and his soul passed into the hereafter.

The killer was elated, more than ever before. He stood and shouted, "See what I can do. Nobody can stop me. I'm invincible." He had almost forgotten the elation he felt after the other murders. He stood there and shuddered as a thrill pulsed through his body. He threw Raymond's rifle in a briar bush and carried Raymond's body to his car. After stuffing Raymond's body in the trunk, he drove to the farm and repeated the process. He needed a reminder of the occasion. Raymond's pocket knife would do nicely. After he placed the nickels on Raymond's eyes, he stripped down to the waist, cut three slashes across his chest with Raymond's knife. Leaning over the grave, he let his blood drip into the grave. He was so excited he danced a little jig around the grave. As he danced, he started singing, "Who's next? Who's next? I can hardly wait. Who's next? Who's next, to meet their deserving fate?"

In May of 63, the strangler had spent the day shopping in Huntington, West Virginia. On his way home, the desire to kill welled up inside him. He decided to cross the bridge into Ohio. On US 52, he drove past Burton Creek but something compelled him to turn around. As he turned on Burton Creek, his heart rate increased and he knew he was near his next victim.

Tom Castle was next. Tom was a farmer and usually worked from before sun up until after sunset. The killer was losing the elation he felt over the last four killings. It had been over a month and he needed that adrenaline rush. He murdered four people and no one knew anything about him. All the people he murdered were written up in the papers as missing. He was beyond reproach, no one would suspect him. Thinking he could do this the rest of his life kept his life juices flowing.

Tom Castle had been putting in long hours getting a field ready for planting. He was working a piece of bottom land out on Burton Creek, about twenty acres. Tom had finished for the night and was coming out the gate on his tractor when a car pulled to a stop about twenty feet past the gate. Someone got out with a flashlight, walked to the front of the car and raised the hood. Tom, being the Good Samaritan, got off the tractor and walked up to see if he could help. That was Tom's last act of kindness. When he leaned over the engine compartment, the killer dropped the flash light and encircled Tom's neck with powerful hands. After he strangled Tom, he felt the excitement return. He dropped Tom to the ground and stood there shuddering violently as his eyes rolled back in his head.

He was so overcome with pleasure, he almost passed out. After stuffing Tom's body in the trunk of his car, he repeated the same procedure as the other four murders.

Two months later, Ed Hopkins was the next victim. He had been plucked from a city street and no one saw or heard a thing. It was late evening and Ed was out for a stroll, bothering no one. Approaching a vacant lot on Chesapeake Avenue in South Point, Ed was lost in thought. Overgrown weeds concealed the strangler, even though he was only three feet from the edge of the road. As Ed walked past, the strangler emerged from the weeds and quietly slipped up behind him. Ed did not have a chance as those powerful hands encircle his throat. Although Ed struggled violently, it was useless. The strangler used the cover of darkness to hide the task of moving the body. He drove to the family farm and repeated the same procedure as the other victims, nickels on the eyes and a memento of the occasion.

Somehow, this murder was not fulfilling to him. He had murdered six people and killing Ed did not give him the feeling of elation he experienced with the other five. All these people were gone from the face of the earth and no one knew them other than missing persons. He wanted the world to know he was a force to be dealt with. His next victims would be left where they could be seen so the world would know of his handiwork.

PART 3

Chapter 1

I left June standing on the curb in front of the newspaper office. She was a reporter for a Cleveland, Ohio newspaper. She and I had a relationship over the last few years. If she only knew how much I wanted to be with her, she could hear my heart screaming, turn around you fool, go back to her. That could not be as I didn't have the luxury of a relationship. My job prevented a permanent relationship with anyone. No woman could live a man, never knowing where he was or even if he was alive. That would put an unbearable strain on any relationship and that was why it best I ride off into the darkness.

I left the darkness of Cleveland, Ohio and headed the beast south. What I affectionately called the beast was my motorcycle. It was my ride for the last year or so while I was working undercover as a narcotics officer. My objective was to reach my hometown of Ironton, Ohio as quickly as possible. After two and a half hours of riding in the dark, I was tired and pulled into a motel on the outskirts of Chillicothe, Ohio. It was another two hours home and the wind tearing at my body compelled me to seek refuge. The last few weeks of my assignment had been extremely tiring and stressful. After I shut the bike off, I walked up to the motel office and saw a sign that read, Ring Bell for Service.

I pushed the bell and immediately heard a loud, Ding-Dong. No one answered the bell so I rang it again. Just as I was getting ready to ring it a third time, I noticed a light come on in a hallway behind the office. A door opened and someone turned a light on in the office. A woman in a ratty looking robe plodded over to the door. After opening it a crack, she asked, “Yeah, what do you want?”

“I’m sorry to bother you, Ma’am, but I’d like to rent a room.”

She didn’t appear to be real happy that I disturbed her sleep and replied, “Aw man, can’t you come back in the morning?”

“Ma’am, I’m beat. I’d really need to get some sleep. If you rent me a room, I’ll give you a fifty dollar tip.”

Her eyes kind of lit up and she asked, “What’s your name, mister?”

“Jack Stevens. I’m just passing through. I’m tired and I really need to sleep for a few hours.”

“Well Mr. Stevens, why are you dressed like that?”

“Because I ride a motorcycle,” I explained as she eyed my leather gear from head to toe.

She had a look of fear in her eyes when I made that statement and asked,

“You’re not going to give me any trouble are you?”

“No Ma’am, I’ll be as quiet as a church mouse.”

She looked me over for a couple of minutes before she slid the safety chain off the catch and allowed me to enter the office. As I signed the register, I noticed she was an attractive woman and for a few seconds I had impure thoughts about her. I thought to myself, Jack, a six pack of beer and a woman would kill you right now. Keep your mind out of your pants. I paid her the room rate and gave her the fifty dollar tip, which she quickly stuck in her robe.

After pushing my bike over to the room, I unpacked a change of clothes and entered the room. The furniture appeared fairly new and the room was clean. I undressed and jumped in the shower. As I let the water cascade down my body, I thought of Barbara. The nights we spent together, before she was shot down by a drug dealer, still haunted me. Her memory was so vivid; I could almost see her standing before me. When the water started turning cold, I stepped out of the shower and wrapped myself in a robe that was hanging on the back of the door. A bright light filled the room and a vision of Barbara appeared before me. She was dressed in white and a golden aura surrounded her. As I reached out to her, my hand touched the aura and warmth started at my finger tips and spread through my body. She extended her hand and led me from the bathroom. I felt as though my feet were not touching the floor. We moved to the bed and I lay down. Barbara looked down at me and smiled as I opened my arms. She lay in the crook of my arm and a serene feeling spread from the top of my head to bottom of my feet. I whispered,

"I miss you, Barbara." Her lips did not move, but the words she spoke were clearly audible.

"I miss you to, Jack. Someday, we will be together again. Until then, you still have work to do. Just remember, my love, I'll always be with you."

A loud knock on the door startled me and Barbara started fading. "Wait sweetheart, please don't go."

"I must, for now, but I'll be back. My love for you is always."

The incessant knocking on the door was getting louder. I shook myself and jumped out of bed. When I opened the door, there stood the desk clerk in that ratty robe.

"What's going on in there?" she asked. "Is the room on fire?"

"No Ma'am, why would you ask a question like that?"

"Well, I was getting ready to go back to bed, when I looked out the window and saw your room was lit up like a forest fire. There was a white light coming from under the door and around the windows. What was it?"

"I don't know Ma'am. I was in the shower and came out when you started banging on the door. I had the television on, maybe the screen went white." If I told her what really happened, she would think I was loony.

"You ain't doing anything illegal in there, are you?"

"No Ma'am, you can come in and look if you like."

"No, that's not necessary. Just so everything is okay in there."

"Everything is just fine, Ma'am," I replied.

After closing the door, I walked back to the bed and lay down. No matter how hard I wished for it, Barbara did not reappear. Just before I drifted off to sleep, I heard her voice again, “I’ll be with you always.”

Saturday morning, I checked out of the room and thanked the lady again for renting me the room. In the light of day and without that ratty robe she was a very attractive woman. The second thing I noticed about her was a wedding ring. Jack Stevens may be a dog, but I draw the line at married women. Husbands are a strange breed. You just never know what they are capable of and I didn’t want to become a statistic.

Chapter 2

Around noon, after pulling into Ironton, I placed a call to Juan Sanchez, Chief of the Ironton Police Department. Juan was the one that got me into the undercover work in the first place. Sometimes, I didn't know I should thank him or kick his rear end. The desk Sergeant put me through to Juan. "Juan, this is Jack. How are you?"

"Jack, it's good to hear from you. Where are you?"

"In my apartment on Center Street."

"Jeez Jack, when did you get in? You know you're still a wanted man? You better lay low the rest of the day until I get your record cleaned up and tell our guys you're okay. I'll stop by your place after work, we need to talk."

"What about, Juan?"

"I'll tell you when I get there. Dickerson will be with me."

"Is that bad attitude back in town?"

"Oh yeah, we'll talk later today, okay?"

"Okay," I replied.

After hanging up the phone, I dialed my brother's phone number. "Hey Jerry, it's your long lost brother, Jack. I'll be by later this evening to see you."

"Where in the hell have you been, Jack? Do you know

it's been almost a year since I heard from you? It's about time you called. You know Mom is getting up in years What if something happened while you were gone? How in the hell would I have gotten in touch with you?"

"Easy brother, I apologize for not staying in touch but I was quite busy and often wondered if I was going to make it through the assignment."

"What in the hell do you mean, assignment? Are you doing the undercover crap again?" he asked.

"Yeah, I was, but I'm not doing it now. I want to come up and soothe over feelings I knew would be bad because I didn't let you know where I was or what I was doing."

"What time you going to be here," he asked?

"Around 9:00 o'clock."

Juan Sanchez and Lt. Dickerson showed up at my door around 7:00 o'clock. Dickerson, always the bad attitude, spoke first, "Hello, little man, I mean Jack. How are you? You did a great job on the Cleveland drug operation. Tony was on our list for several years. It seemed like every time we sent in an operative, he would get discovered and end up floating face down in Lake Erie."

"Damn you Dickerson, now is a hell of a time to be telling me that. If I'd known that before, I may have told you to kiss my ass."

"Take it easy Jack, I had confidence in you. I figured you could get nasty enough to get the job done."

"Thanks for the vote of confidence," I replied sarcastically.

"Don't get all spastic on me Jack." replied Dickerson. "I gave you a good cover story and I helped your ass out of a few tight spots. The only thing you need to do is buy a watch and learn how to tell time."

"Don't need one," I replied, "as long as I have your phone number."

Juan broke in, "All right guys, let's can it. We have something important to discuss."

I quit bickering with Dickerson and told Juan, "Sorry, but my manners have been lacking for the last several months. What do you have?"

Dickerson continued the conversation, "We've had four murders in the last six months. My own personal opinion is that it's the work of a serial killer."

"What makes you think it's a serial killer?"

"Each victim had nickels placed on their eyes, that plus a gut feeling."

Juan spoke up, "I think its two killers, and one is just a copy cat."

"Why?" I replied.

Juan continued, "Most of the killings were committed by different means. Two were strangled, one was shot, and one was stabbed multiple times. I think the strangulations are by the same person and I think the shooting and the stabbing are copy cats with the nickels on the eyes. But I still think they're connected some way. Jack, do you think you might be able to snoop around and see if you can find out anything?"

"I'd be glad to, but I'm still a wanted man, according to the Ironton PD."

"I took care of that right after you called this morning," replied Juan. "Your record has been cleared and I told all the local police officers that you're not a fugitive anymore. Several of them asked why. I told them you were on an undercover assignment for the last year or so. After I told everyone, your old partner, Don Hamilton, stood and started applauding. Soon every officer in the station was standing and applauding right along with Don."

"Okay, guys, I'll see what I can find out. I'll need all the information you have on the victims. I also want any incidents over the last five years that matches the same MO. I don't think you're going to find any with a matching MO for the coins on the eyes so let's start with the MO on the strangulations."

Juan agreed to get me everything they had. In my opinion, that many murders in such a short time had to have a common thread. It would be my chore to find that thread.

Around 8:30 PM, I called my brother and told him I was on the way. I straddled the beast and pointed it in the direction of South Point. It felt good to be out in the wind without having to look over my shoulder. No more worries about hiding from the cops. As I started south on Third Street, a police car fell in behind me. After a half mile, the red light started flashing. Being the law abiding citizen I am, I pulled to the curb. The car door opened and footsteps started towards me.

"Jack, is that you?"

"Yes, I'm Jack. Who are you?"

"It's me, Don."

I turned in the saddle to see my old partner standing there, grinning like a possum eating briars. Don approached and gave me a hearty hand shake and a slap on the back.

"Damn Jack, its sure good to see you. When Sanchez told us what you were doing for the last year or so, I wasn't surprised. You were to good a cop to go bad. All the guys, at the station, are proud of you."

"I appreciate the kind words, Don, but I didn't do anymore than anyone else, given the same circumstances. You guys fighting the battle everyday are the heroes."

"Boy, it's good to see you, Jack. Are you coming back to the station?"

"Yeah, I'll be back in uniform on Monday."

After Don and I talked for a while, he said he had to be getting back on patrol. I rode up to my brother's house and we had a good time catching up. I finally told him what I'd been doing for the last year or so. Jerry told me, "It's a good thing I didn't know the whole story, I might have been a lot more worried than I was."

"I'll tell you what, Jerry, there was a time or two I thought you might end up being an only child." As we continued our visit, Jerry filled me in on family. Mom was still in Columbus, Ohio and getting along great. She and

Aunt Charlene were doing what made them happy; flea markets, church, and shopping. I missed John, but I felt good that the person responsible for his death was burning in hell. John was in a better place; no tears and no sorrow. Streets of gold sounded a whole hell of a lot better than the mean streets I'd been traveling lately. We talked until after midnight and Jerry told me,

"You might as well spend the night here."

Sunday morning, after everyone arose, we continued to catch up on each others lives.

I left Jerry's house around 4:00 PM and headed back down the highway. After pulling off the highway at Coal Grove, I headed north on Third street. My stomach was growling and that was my cue to pull into Moore's Restaurant to get a bite to eat. After parking the beast, I went inside and sat at the counter. I became aware of someone looking at me. When you've lived like I had for the last year or so, you can sense when you are being watched. Looking around, I saw a young lady looking at me and when she walked over, the first thing I noticed were her deep blue eyes. She looked familiar, but I could not put a name to the face. When she came over to take my order, I suddenly remembered her name. "Hi Rebecca, how are you?"

"Do I know you?" she replied.

"I'm Jack, Jack Stevens."

"Jack, it is you. You've changed. You've lost a lot of weight, which I think I found," she said as she patted her rear end.

"Yeah, I've lost a little. You look good, Rebecca. You were always to skinny in high school. Life must be treating you right. What are you up to these days?"

"I work here in the evening and go to school during the day."

"What are you taking and when do you find time to fit it in?"

"I'm taking business administration and have about six more months to get my degree. It's been a little rough at times. Seems all I do is sleep, eat and go to school. Most of my classes are late mornings so the evening work fits my schedule. What are you doing, Jack?"

"I kind of travel a lot for several organizations. I guess you could say I'm a trouble shooter. Sometimes, I'm gone for quite a while."

"That sounds interesting and secretive. You'll have to tell me about it sometime. See anything on the menu you like?"

"Well, I see something I like but I don't think it's on the menu."

Rebecca replied, "You never know Jack, sometimes you just have to ask for it but until then what do you want to eat?"

"How about a burger and fries," I replied.

After eating, I paid my tab and walked out. Rebecca was standing out by the curb and I walked over and asked her, "What are you doing out here? I thought you worked the evening shift."

"One of the girls was sick today; I came in early to cover for her. The boss has someone coming in to cover the rest of my shift. Right now, I'm waiting on a taxi. This time of the day they take forever to get here."

"If you want, Rebecca, I'll give you a ride home."

She looked at me for a few seconds and said, "Okay, thanks."

We walked over to the beast and I straddled it and told her to hop on.

"Wow Jack, you really have changed."

Rebecca hiked up her skirt and hopped on behind me, flashing some shapely legs in the process. She lived in the 1000 block of South Seventh Street and when we pulled up at her house, I shut the bike off. When she dismounted, more beautiful leg was shown. I sat there a few minutes talking to her before she asked, "Are you coming in?"

"Are you inviting me in?"

Her one word reply, "Yes."

When we walked into the apartment, she asked if I'd like something to drink.

"Yes please, beer, soda, water, whatever you got."

She went to the kitchen and returned with a couple of sodas and we spent a while talking about high school days. She turned on the radio and one of my favorite songs was playing I stood and reached for Rebecca's hand. She timidly placed her hand in mine and stood slowly. As we danced, she laid her head on my shoulder and her body molded to mine. Her thighs brushed mine as we danced around the room. With my arm around her waist, I could feel her lithe, supple body flowing from step to step. As Rebecca looked up at me with those deep blue eyes, I leaned down and put my lips on hers. When my tongue parted her lips, I could feel the tremors of anticipation coursing through our bodies. Gently, I placed kisses on her face and let my lips slide down to her throat.

Rebecca was panting quite rapidly as I unbuttoned her blouse. After I slid it off her shoulders, I placed my lips on the soft flesh between her breasts. Hand in hand, we walked into the bedroom and as we undressed each other, our breath was coming in gasps. I gently placed her on the bed and began to explore her body with my lips. As I teased one breast then the other, I felt a tingling going up my arms, making the hair stand on my arms and the back of my neck. I brought her fingers to my lips and kissed each one. When I neared her wrists, I detected an aroma that dreams were made of. I tasted her wrists and let my lips glide up her arm to the hollow of her elbow. As I caressed her arms with my lips, I gently caressed her breasts with my fingers. Gently squeezing her nipples elicited moans from deep inside her throat. Rising above her, I kissed her face and slowly let my lips slide lower on her body. When I kissed her breasts, she began pushing her femininity up to meet me. When I slid lower on her torso, she forcibly held me against her body. As I ran my tongue in lazy circles on her body, Rebecca started pushing violently against me. When I rose above her again and prepared to enter her femininity, she raised her hips to meet me. As we slowly thrust against each other, a desire was building in us that could only culminate in an explosion of feelings. Faster and faster, deeper and deeper until we both were spent. As we lay side by side, I continued to explore her body. Around 10:00 PM, I arose, got dressed and kissed her one more time before leaving.

Chapter 3

I fired up the beast and headed home. That evening was something I'd remember for a long time. Rebecca's nude body was etched in my memory. Monday morning, after reporting in at the station, I was partnered with Don Hamilton, my old partner. Sanchez told me I would only be in uniform a few days, and then I would be working under the direct supervision of Dickerson, a Federal Agent. Don and I made the rounds for a few days. We ran in a couple of drunks and stopped a guy for inoperable brake lights. The car was a beat up old trap and the driver looked suspicious as hell. We gave him a warning ticket and told him to get the stop lights fixed. When we got back in the patrol car, I asked Don, "Didn't he look suspicious to you?"

"Yeah, he did, but we can't hold him because he looked suspicious."

"I know, Don, but that son of a bitch gave me the willies. He was eerie as hell. I hope I don't ever run into him again. Let's call the station and have them run his plates to see if anything pops up."

"Okay," he replied, "but I don't think we'll come up with

anything. Damn Jack, since you've been undercover, you seem to see the worst in everyone."

"I know, but I learned a lot about reading people. If you expect to survive, you have to do it and do it fast."

Don called the station and asked them to run the plate, Z-3916-R.

When we finished the shift, we went to Juan's office to find out about the license plate number. Juan told us, "All we found out was the owner's name, Winton Craig. No wants or warrants and he resides in Hecla, Ohio.

"I tell you Juan, that guy was strange."

"Don't worry about him," Juan replied. "Don will keep an eye out for him. You have to report to Dickerson on Monday."

Don and I ran normal patrol for the rest of the week.

8:00 AM, Monday morning; I walked in Dickerson's office. "Good morning Arvin. How are you?"

"Why in the hell did you call me by my first name?"

"Now-Now, Arvin. Don't get testy. You call me by my first name all the time. Don't you like your first name?"

"Hell no, call me Dickerson."

"Okay Arv... I mean Dickerson. What have you got on the murders?"

"It's all here in the folders, ages, names, addresses, method by which they were killed, and the coroner's autopsy report for each body. Dickerson tossed the folders to me and said, "You can use that desk over there," as he pointed to it.

I walked over and sat down and started going through the folders. There were four folders for the victims and three more that matched to MO of the strangler.

The first folder I looked at was for Marie Iverson, a house wife from Ironton, Ohio. The cause of death was a gunshot to the back. The bullet hit a main artery and she bled to death in a matter of minutes. No other marks were on the body. The second victim was Allan Jennings, an architect from Ironton. He was strangled and the picture of the body showed dark bruises on his throat. The third victim was William Hannon of Coal Grove, Ohio. He too, was strangled and had the same kind of bruises on his throat. The fourth victim was a hobo, called John Doe because no one ever claimed the body. He was found by the rail road tracks, not very far from the rail road station. His murder was the most vicious; eighteen stab wounds with one that pierced his heart. The only thing the murders had in common were the nickels on the eyes.

I knew many years ago, coins were placed on the eyes of the dead to keep the eyelids closed. Was the killer unable to look the victims in the eyes after he killed them? Was there a meaning to the nickels or were they used just to confuse the authorities. The nickels were even listed as to the mint years. Did the mint years have any significance? Why not pennies or some other coin? Why nickels? My work was cut out for me and I didn't know if I was up to the challenge.

My first step was to re-interview the victim's families. I

would start with Widow Jennings, wife of Allan. I pulled out of the office on Monday afternoon, around 5:30, and headed for Widow Jennings' house. I did not call first as I wanted gut reactions to my questions. I did not want to give them time to think about their answers. Sometimes, the best and most truthful answers are the ones just blurted out. If a person has the time to think about an answer, they tend to leave out important details and I needed details.

I pulled up in front of Widow Jennings' house around 6:00 PM. When I knocked on the door, a classy looking lady, appearing to be fifty or so, opened the door. "Yes, may I help you?"

"Mrs. Jennings, my name is Jack Stevens with the Ohio State Police. I've recently been assigned to your husband's case." After I showed her my badge, I asked, "Do you mind if I come in? I won't take up much of your time."

"Come in, please," she replied.

After going in, we walked to the kitchen. She said she had something cooking and didn't want it to burn.

"Mrs. Jennings, you've probably been asked these questions many times before, but since I'm new on the case, I would like to ask some of them again, okay?"

"Anything to find the person that took my Allan away from me. If you find him, I hope he gets the electric chair and he rots in hell."

"Mrs. Jennings," I replied, "It's not if we find him, but rather when we find him."

She gave me a half smile as if to say, it's been quite a while and no one has made any headway in finding the killer.

"Mrs. Jennings, did Allan ever talk to you about having any trouble with anyone at his job?"

"No sir, he was a very friendly man and well respected in his profession."

"Did he ever stop anywhere after work for, maybe, a drink?"

"Sometimes, he would stop at the Latin Quarter after work for a drink. We might eat there a couple of times a month."

I didn't ask her but I couldn't figure why anyone with class would be stopping at the Latin Quarter.

"Mrs. Jennings, a lot of the other questions were answered in the original report. Is there anything else you would like to tell me?"

"No," she replied.

"I do have one more question and I don't know how to ask it but to come right out with it."

"What's that," she replied?

"Was your husband faithful to you?"

She looked at me for a few seconds. I saw her face turning red and she told me to get the hell out. In my opinion, she took to long to think about the question. If he was faithful she should have simply said yes. I couldn't fathom why she reacted like that. I needed to check his fidelity and the first thing that came to mind was a jealous husband was responsible for his death. Although, Mrs. Jennings was taller than most women, she looked kind of frail. I didn't think she had the power to strangle anyone. I thought of an old adage I heard every now and then; Hell hath no fury like a woman scorned. I'd check with Don to see if there had been any domestic violence calls at the Jennings' household. I filed those thoughts away for a while as Allan Jennings was a big man and it would have taken a person of strength overcome him.

The folders for the MO matches showed three persons used the method of strangulation over the last five years.

#1 Alvin Leroy Thompson of Chillicothe, Ohio AKA Roy Alvin, Al Thomas

#2 John Wayne Simpson of Portsmouth, Ohio AKA Duke Simpson

#3 Orville Robert Adams of Ashland, Kentucky AKA Bob Orr

After checking with the Ohio State Pen, Thompson and Simpson were still serving time. A call to the Summitt Correctional Facility revealed that Adams was paroled about a year ago. His conviction had been for attempted murder and he served four years of a six year sentence. The Correctional Facility gave me the name of his parole officer; Harold Austin. After contacting Austin and getting his address, I was off to 360 Belle Road in Westwood, Kentucky. No one would answer my incessant knocking so I peeked in the windows. As I was walking around the house, looking in the windows, a neighbor, Mrs. Eva

Greenwood, came out and told me "Mr. Adams moved."

"Mrs. Greenwood, how long did Adams live in the house?"

"About a year, I think. He never was one to say much. I think he might have been in some sort of trouble at one time."

"What makes you think that Ma'am?"

"A few times, over the last year or so, I saw a Department of Corrections vehicle stop at his house. Some mean looking man would get out and go in the house. He would stay for an hour or so."

"Did Mr. Adams ever say anything to you about these visits?"

"No, like I said, we didn't talk much."

"Mrs. Greenwood, when you did talk to him, what did you talk about?"

"It was generally about the weather or some other trivial subject."

"Do you remember when he moved out?"

"It was about a month ago."

"Did he happen to say why he was moving or where he was going?"

"The only thing he said was that he couldn't afford the rent and that he found someplace cheaper."

"Did he say where?"

"No, but you might be able to find out through the U-haul place."

"Why, is that where he worked?"

"No, that was what he moved in. I believe he was a mechanic and worked at a gas station in Flatwoods."

"Thank you, Mrs. Greenwood, you've been a big help."

After leaving Westwood, I stopped at the local U-haul store and inquired about a rental in the name of Orville Adams. The store manager, Alex Hooper, told me he would have to send the request to the office and get back to me in a couple of days. All receipts and monies were sent to the office on a weekly basis. After returning to Ironton, I called the parole officer and asked him, "Do you know Adams moved?"

"No I didn't, Jack. That means Mr. Adams violated his parole and when I find him He will go back to the pen."

"Well," I told him, "I'm working on a lead and if anything comes of it, I'll let you know."

Two days later, I received a call from Alex, the U-haul manager. He said, "Mr. Stevens, I got that information you requested. Adams rented a truck, one way, from Ashland to Olive Hill, Kentucky."

"Thanks Alex, I appreciate the information." The next morning, I hopped on the beast and headed for Olive Hill. After finding the U-haul dealer, I inquired about Adams. The dealer remembered him but did not know where he moved. I left there and went to the electric company and got a list of the new electric hook ups for the last few months. When I called Austin, the PO, he agreed to meet me the next morning to help check out the list. Austin and I met at a local coffee shop and started going over the list.

None of the new service orders were listed in the name of Adams so we had the job of checking out each one. We hit pay dirt. The name listed on one of the orders was Joe Stefan and he was home. Mr. Stefan rented the house a few months ago and put an ad in the local paper for a room mate. Adams answered the ad and Stefan rented the room to Adams. He also told us that Adams was working at a gas station in town. We returned to town and found the station and Austin identified a person pumping gas as Adams. Adams accompanied us back to Ironton where he underwent intense questioning. When I asked him why he moved, he said. "I couldn't afford the rent in Westwood and I had a cousin tell me I could get a job at a gas station in Olive Hill. I'm only paying half as much rent as I was in Westwood." His parole officer spoke up, "Why didn't you tell me you were moving?"

"I did,' he replied, "I called and your secretary said she would tell you."

Austin immediately called his secretary and asked her about Adams. I could almost hear her answer. "OOPS," asked Austin, "What in the hell do you mean oops? We'll talk about this when I get back."

When I talked to Adams, I got the feeling he was not the one I was looking for. He said he had been in Olive Hill a little over a month. The murders were committed before he left the area but still felt he just wasn't the one I called his land lord and he verified that Adams was in Olive Hill for a little over a month and had been working twelve hours a days, seven days a week. Since Adams didn't own a car, I just didn't think he could have covered the distance involved to commit the murders, even from Westwood. The parole officer told Adams he would have to get approval before any future moves. The PO took Adams back to Olive Hill and I vowed to keep Adams in the back of my mind for a while.

Chapter 4

After Parole Officer Austin left, my next stop was my apartment. As a result of my talk with Widow Jennings, I had to check out the Latin Quarter and I needed to get out of these street clothes into my biker gear. After changing, I fired up the beast and rolled up to the Latin Quarter. From the number of cars in the parking lot, the place had to be packed. When I walked in, I was shocked. The place had changed. Men in suits and ladies in elegant dresses were seated around tables enjoying their evening meal. Even the bartender was wearing a white shirt and tie. The biker gear just did not fit in and I did not feel very comfortable being there with everyone staring at me. As I turned to leave, I met a young couple coming in. They were dressed to the nines and the guy snickered at me. I guess he was trying to impress his lady. I wasn't in a cordial mood and asked him, "What the hell are you snickering at?"

"Your kind is no longer welcome here," he replied as he snickered again.

"Tell you what asshole, my kind will drag your ass out of here and kick it all over the parking lot."

This time he snorted real loud and gave me the finger. Just as I was about to grab him, he ducked behind his lady. "Go ahead, tough guy. Hide behind her skirt, at least she didn't flinch. Listen punk, if you were on fire, I wouldn't even piss on you to put it out. Now get out of my sight."

He took off for the dining room and left the lady standing there. I addressed the young lady, "I'm sorry Ma'am. I didn't mean to frighten you. I've been out of town for a while and didn't know the Latin Quarter had been turned into a respectable place."

As I turned to leave, she said, "Wait a minute, I wasn't frightened."

She pulled a scrap of paper out of her purse and scribbled something on it. "Call me sometime." When she handed me the paper, I noticed a wedding ring on her finger. I took the note and walked out the door. Once outside, I tore up the paper and scattered it in the wind. Jack Stevens may be a dog, but he doesn't fraternize with married women. As I walked out to the beast, I wondered, if that was his wife, what kind of an excuse he could give for his cowardice. Maybe that wasn't his wife. Maybe his wife was sitting home all alone. As a matter of fact, maybe her husband was sitting home all alone.

Straddling the beast, I headed north on Third Street. As I neared the Tug and Hug, I decided to pull in and get a beer. Everything seemed the same as the last time I was in there. The bar, the poolroom, even the bartender was the same as before. After a half hour, I decided to move on. On the way out, I accidentally bumped a patron coming in. He didn't take kindly to the accident and I was not in a kindly mood after the fiasco at the Latin Quarter. "Watch it asshole," he said.

"I'm sorry man; I didn't mean to bump into you. I apologize."

"You better apologize, asshole. I may have to kick you ass."

That remark was just enough to put me at the boiling point. "Listen pal, you may try but you better pack a lunch because it's going to be an all day job. I said I was sorry. I'm through talking about it. If you want to fight, I'll take you outside and mop up the street with your punkin head."

That kind of pissed him off and he started to take a swing at me. Before he could finish his swing, I popped him between the eyes and he staggered for a few seconds. I grabbed the back of his head and smashed his face against the door jamb.

Marie Iverson was next on my list. When she was alive, she lived in north Ironton with her husband. Her husband answered the door and I explained who I was. "Mr. Iverson, may I have a few minutes of your time?"

"Please, come in. Would you like a cup of coffee?"

"No thanks, I just need to ask a few questions."

Before I could ask any questions, he started remembering the night it happened. "You know, I retired a few years ago and Marie was looking forward to retiring in a couple of years. We were regular church goers and Marie went to church that night. She was shot on the way home. I wasn't feeling good that night and Marie went to church alone. When she didn't come home on time, I was concerned about her. I called the church and when no one answered, I was worried and called the police. They found her about an hour later out on Ox Road. She had been shot in the back. The bullet hit a main artery and she bled to death right there in the car. The motor was still running"

"Mr. Iverson, did Marie have any run ins with anyone you know of?"

"No, Marie was the sweetest person on earth. I really miss her. I don't know how long I can go on without her."

Mr. Iverson broke down and started crying and was just too distraught to continue the questioning, so I packed up and left.

Tuesday back at the office, I studied the files all day. Somewhere, there had to be something that would tie these murders together. If they were the work of a serial killer, I needed to find a common thread. Another thought entered my mind as I sat there analyzing the files. If this was the work of one person, he or she would have to be insane. An insane person that kills for no rhyme or reason would be most difficult to apprehend. That person would have to make a big mistake to be caught. The two clues we had were, the nickels and a 38 slug pulled from Marie's body. Around 5:00 o'clock, I told Dickerson,

"I'm going home, my brain is tired."

"Okay Jack," he replied, "I'll see you tomorrow."

That night, my dreams were violent. In my dreams, I could see a person committing the murders. As I tried to prevent each murder, it was like I was moving in slow motion while every one else was in super speed. The knife, the gun, and the person's hands were clearly visible. The look of agony on the victims' faces, as they drew their last breath, would haunt me for the rest of my life. The face of the killer was the only one not in focus. There seemed to be a shroud of fog over his face.

Wednesday morning, I drove to Coal Grove to talk to the widow of William Hannon. After talking to Mrs. Hannon, she could not add anymore than what was in the report. Mr. Hannon's body was found on the banks of the Ohio River. He had been missing for several days when the body was found. A thorough search of the river bank turned up his gear about a mile north of the spot his body washed up. Two nickels were found near his gear. The consensus was that he had been killed at that spot and his body placed in the river as there wasn't any water in his lungs. After the autopsy, strangulation was ruled as the cause of death. While the bruise marks on his neck were not as vivid as Alan Jennings, they were still there. After a few days in the water, the marks had started to fade. His body was found by another fisherman who noticed a strange odor, started nosing around and discovered the body with his left foot tangled in some brush at the water's edge. Nothing in the report, although it was fairly complete, connected him to the other victims.

The John Doe was the most violent murder of all. He had been stabbed eighteen times, one of the stab wounds piercing the heart. He had not been identified in the three months since his death. The person who did this was undoubtedly insane. The body had been discovered on the railway right of way; about a hundred yards from the river bank. The proximity of the river to John Doe and Hannon being found on the river bank was a common thread, a very thin one to say the least. Jennings and Hannon were strangled, again a common thread. Iverson was shot. The only thing common to all four were the nickels.

Wednesday afternoon, I started visiting the crime scenes. A vacant lot on North Tenth Street, the murder scene out on Ox Road, the Ohio river bank, and the railroad tracks about a half mile south of the train station got my attention. Each of the locations proved to be eerie. There were bad feelings coming at me from all directions. When I visited the Ox Road murder scene, it was especially eerie as I envisioned Marie Iverson begging for her life. My hair was standing on end and my skin was clammy. All of a sudden, a voice interrupted my thoughts, "Jack, I'm here" and I turned to see who it camc from. No one was there. I drew my weapon and asked, "Who's there?" No one answered and then I heard the voice again. "Jack, turn to your left."

I turned to my left to find the source of the voice and still did not see anyone. I was concerned about being out in the open and not knowing who was out there.

"Who's there?" I asked again.

"Jack, it's me Barbara. Walk towards my voice."

I started walking and went in a straight line for several hundred feet. Then I heard her voice again.

"Jack, stop here. This is where you'll find what you're seeking."

I didn't know what the hell I was looking for as I began to search under bushes and fallen trees. After about forty five minutes, I was about ready to give up. I sat against a tree and in frustration; I picked up a rock and threw it. When it hit the ground, it rang out with a sharp metallic sound. Jumping up and running over to the area, I began running my hands along the ground, scooting leaves and debris out of the way. I was ready to give up again when my fingers touched a hard object. After carefully removing the debris, sticking out of the ground, about a half inch, was a gun barrel. Being careful not to touch it, I dug it out and picked it up by inserting a stick down the barrel. If it had fingerprints on it, I didn't want to smudge them. As I got back to the car, I heard Barbara's voice again,

"I miss you Jack."

"I miss you too, Barbara."

I wrapped the pistol, a 38 snub nose revolver, in some paper I found on the ground and headed back to the State Police Office. As soon as I walked in, I asked Dickerson to have the lab check for finger prints and run a ballistic test on it.

"Where did you find that gun, Jack?"

"Out near the crime scene on Ox Road."

"That's where Marie Iverson was shot, wasn't it?" replied Dickerson.

"Yeah, if the killings were done by the same person, it might be a strong lead, especially if we can get some fingerprints from it."

"How in the hell did you find it? We went all through those woods."

"Dickerson, you wouldn't believe me if I told you. Let's just say I had an angel looking over my shoulder."

"Whatever you say Jack. If that's the gun that killed Iverson, we just got our first break. We'll know after we check the gun for finger prints and ballistics"

Dickerson called Agent Steve Owen in the office.

"Steve, take this gun to the Columbus lab. Have it checked for finger prints and have them do a ballistics test. We think it has some connection to Marie Iverson. Plan on spending the night and tell them it's a rush job."

"What if they don't have the report ready by Thursday afternoon?"

"Steve, this is important. I need the reports ASAP. If you have to stay Thursday night, you have an expense account, use it."

"Okay, boss. I'll give you a call as soon as I get the results."

Steve called us Friday morning and said it was the gun that killed Iverson. The sad thing was the gun had been wiped clean of all finger prints, except for a partial on the trigger and the lab said it was not enough to get a match.

Saturday was my day off but I could not sit around my apartment doing nothing. In the late afternoon, I walked the few blocks to the John Doe murder scene. Walking south, past the railroad station, I was soon at the spot where the body was found. Looking to my left, I saw nothing but vacant buildings. Unless someone happened by, a murder could take place here and only the murderer would know about it. I sat on the tracks and gazed at the vacant building across the street. I was saddened that John Doe died here and no one gave a damn.

I spoke aloud, "John Doe, your death will be avenged."

When I arose to leave, I felt an urgent need to cross the street. Walking up and down in front of the buildings caused edginess in me. Something evil happened here besides the John Doe murder. I could not shake the feeling as I waded through the weeds and debris to the store fronts. The doors were locked and the windows were painted over. There were several places where the paint had flaked off over the years and when I peered in the windows, I saw nothing but empty littered rooms. After checking several of the buildings, I approached a two story brick building. Something compelled me to go inside. I said out loud, "Barbara, I hope you're looking over my shoulder." After kicking in the front door, the fading sun just filtered in enough to illuminate two big river rats. They were standing on hind legs and it seemed like they were daring me to come in. Even after I hollered at them, they would not move. "Okay guys, you got three seconds to vacate the premises."

Still no movement, so I took out my pistol and fired one time. One dropped dead and the other one took off for a hole in the wall. The dead one would be a meal for the survivor after I left.

After going though the four rooms on the bottom floor, I started up the steps. The stairs creaked and groaned as I walked up. The back part of the second floor was just another littered room. The front room was another story. In the middle of the floor, lay a body. It appeared to be a white male, stripped to the waist; dried blood was all over his chest. Blood splattered the walls and had pooled under his body. It appeared he had been stabbed numerous times. As I stooped to examine him, I got an eerie feeling I was being watched. I grabbed my pistol and whirled around. Something stood in the doorway, crouched as if ready to spring at me. "What the hell are you?" I yelled.

A menacing growl came from deep in its throat and the eyes looking at me appeared red in the dim light. As it started towards me, I backed up against thc blood smeared wall.

"Stop damn you, or I'll shoot." I didn't know what the hell it was but it kept inching towards me. A cold sweat drenched my body and my heart was beating so hard, I thought it was going to pound out of my chest. I was scared as hell and was not going to let that thing lay a hand on me. I fired and the sound pierced the darkness. A moan came from deep in its throat that turned into a howl. Suddenly, it turned and ran for the door. Footsteps echoed in the hall and down the stairs. After I heard the footsteps going out the opened door, I jumped up and ran for the window, rubbing frantically at the grime on the inside of the window. I caught a glimpse of something running across the street; with its left arm hanging limply at its side. I hurried out of the room and down the stairs. I hit the front door and was standing in the middle of the street in a matter of seconds. After I caught my breath, I started looking around and saw several drops of blood on the sidewalk and in the street. I followed the blood trail over to the flood wall and found more blood at the base of the flood wall. Climbing the spikes on the flood wall was an iffy situation, but I had to do it. Seeing blood near the top of the wall, I peeked over the top and saw nothing but river and bushes.

I felt sure I'd run into that thing again, but for the present, I had to call Dickerson.

"Dickerson, this is Jack, get your tail out here, pronto. Bring the County Coroner and some guys to investigate a crime scene."

"Where are you Jack, and what in the hell did you do, kill somebody?"

"No dammit, I didn't kill anyone, just get out here quick. Call Sanchez and tell him to send a couple of men out here."

"I will Jack, but I have to know where you are."

"I'm about a half mile south of the train station on Second Street."

Dickerson, Sanchez, and four city cops showed up about ten minutes later. Dickerson was the first one to speak, "Jack, what the hell is going on?"

"I don't know, but there's a body upstairs, front room. He has been stabbed numerous times, blood smeared all over the wall, bloody foot prints all over the floor. It looks like he's been there more than a day or two. Listen guys, you're going to find this hard to believe, but there was something in there."

Sanchez asked, "What do you mean something?"

"Listen, I'm not crazy, there was something in there that growled and started after me."

"It was probably a dog," replied Dickerson.

"Dog, my ass. That thing walked on two legs and when it growled, it did not sound like a dog. When it kept coming at me, I yelled for it to stop and when it didn't, I shot at it. I must have hit it because there a blood trail leading over to the flood wall. I'd like to go over the flood wall after it, but I sure as hell ain't going alone."

"Damn, I never thought I'd see the day that Jack Stevens was afraid of anything," replied

Dickerson.

"Tell you what asshole, I'd like to see you go over the wall by yourself."

Dickerson shut his mouth as the Coroner pulled up.

The Coroner pulled out a body bag and started in the building. Just as he stepped through the door, he stuck his head back out and told one of the officers to bring a flashlight. Once inside, I heard him say, "Damn, I just about need a body bag for the rat. He's a big one. Just about the biggest I've ever seen." He and his assistant went upstairs and did what coroners do, taking blood samples from the wall and floor, took pictures of the body and carried it out. He said the murder was very similar to John Doe. The last thing he said was, "Oh yeah, nickels on the eyes."

I asked Dickerson if he wanted to accompany me on a trip across the wall.

"Jack, we won't find anything in the dark. We'll get a team together and you can lead them over the wall tomorrow morning."

"I thought so," I replied, under my breath.

"What was that," Dickerson asked?

"I said I hope it doesn't snow."

"Christ Jack, it's the middle of August."

"I know Dickerson. That's why I hope it doesn't snow. It would mess up a beautiful day."

Dickerson walked off, muttering under his breath.

CHAPTER 5

I met with Don Hamilton and Juan Sanchez at the crime scene, Sunday morning around 8:00 o'clock. Don was razing me about being afraid of whatever that thing was.

"Don, if you're so damn brave, let me see you go over the wall first."

"That's okay Jack, You're in charge of this investigation, so you get to go first."

Going hand over hand up the climbing spikes, I reached the top of the flood wall and looked over. After I dropped down to the other side, I yelled for Sanchez and Don to climb over the wall. Soon, we were standing at the base of the wall, trying to decide which direction to go, north or south. For no particular reason, we started south about ten feet apart. About three minutes later, Don said, "Blood on the ground." We picked up the trail and started following it. Since the bushes along that stretch of the Ohio River were sparse, the blood trail was not hard to follow.

We followed the blood trail upriver for another hundred yards. Then, it disappeared into a thicket of bushes about five feet high and thirty feet in diameter. We circled the thicket and couldn't find the blood trail leaving the thicket. There was nothing left to do but go in that tangle of bushes. I took the point where the blood trail entered the thicket. Sanchez and Don were stationed about a third of the way around on each side. As I entered the underbrush, my senses were working overtime. What if that damn thing comes at me, I've got no place to maneuver. Three feet inside the thicket there was more blood. A few more feet of forward progress yielded more blood. About ten feet in, there was a matted down area where it looked like something bedded down for the night. Several splotches of blood were readily apparent. As I looked over the bed area, I noticed a big clump of hair snagged on a limb. "Don, Sanchez, come in here. There's something you have to see." When they worked their way in, I pointed out the bedding area and the clump of hair.

Don spoke up, "Damn, Jack, what have you gotten us into? There's blood all over the place."

Sanchez said, "Let's get samples of the blood and that hair."

We finished in the thicket and started trying to find more blood outside the perimeter. After walking another half mile up river, we found a branch lying at the foot of the flood wall along with a set of foot prints. The foot prints didn't seem to be animal or human because they were almost obscured and pointed away from the wall. It looked like the branch was used to wipe out the foot prints from the thicket to the flood wall. It would take something of reasonable intelligence to cover tracks. Don climbed to the top of the flood wall and didn't see anything unusual. After a futile search for more blood, we headed back to the station. Sanchez said he would take the blood samples and the hair to the state lab to see if he can get it identified...

Monday afternoon, Sanchez called Dickerson and told him, "The blood's human, but we're confused about the hair. The lab said it was definitely not human. I had several other people look at it and they said it looked more like animal fur, most likely wolf. That's what stumps me. We haven't had wolves around here since the early 1900's. I don't know what Jack got into, but I do not like the way it sounds, a frigging wolf man." After Dickerson repeated the conversation to me, I told him, "Call him back, I want to know what they found in that room on Second Street."

"I've got to call the coroner for that." he said,

"Well, call him," I replied.

When he finished talking to the coroner, he turned to me and said, "Human blood and animal hair of some kind."

Tuesday and Wednesday were routine days following up on the body I found in the vacant building. His name was Darrel Wilson. He was a contractor in Ironton and did some youth counseling at a local youth organization. Darrel Wilson was divorced and did not have any children. Several people I talked to said he was a good counselor.

Maybe, by not having children, he could look at a situation and give good advice because he was not influenced with any preconceived ideas about children. When I was finally able to run down his ex-wife, Amanda, she told me he was a violent person when she was married to him. She said he beat her once and that's why she divorced him. I also learned from her that he was dabbling in the occult and even devil worship. Before they divorced, she said he was gone for a few weeks for some kind of military training. I thanked her and went on my way.

Wednesday afternoon, I called Dickerson and told him I was going to the youth organization where Wilson did his counseling. I was met by an elderly woman, Mrs. White, Director of Tri State Youth Services. She told me they provide individual counseling plus family counseling, helped teenagers cope with family stress, helped with job training, and helped secure jobs for their youth. Along with recreational activities and tutoring, they also had mentors for children of single parent homes. Mr. Wilson was a mentor for young boys in their early to late teens.

"Mrs. White, may I look around his office?"

"Since you are with the police, I guess its okay. Just remember, anything you see in there about any of his kids, as we call them, is confidential."

Mr. Wilson's office had many trinkets of a military nature, plus hand carved dolls, tomahawks, and a bow and arrow set. On an opposite wall there was a shield and spear along side a couple of stuffed deer heads. The shield had a pentagram painted on it. I thought, quite the outdoors man. Pulling the chair back, I sat at the desk and started going through the desk drawers. Nothing of interest caught my eye until I checked a bottom drawer. There was a note pad with several boys' names on it. At the top of the pad were the words, Los Lobos. I copied the names and put the list back in the drawer. Lobo is another name for wolf and I wondered if it had any connection to what I saw the other night? I needed help on this one. As I was getting ready to leave, I asked Mrs. White if she could give me some addresses on a few of the kids that came to the center.

"I'm sorry, Mr. Stevens, but those records are confidential."

"Oh well, I'd thought I'd give it a try."

I thanked her and left. I couldn't tell her why I wanted them and I certainly couldn't tell her I could come back with a search warrant. She might decide to hide the records if I divulged that information to her at that time.

Convincing Dickerson and Sanchez would be difficult at best. Trying to convince a Judge would be next to impossible.

"Dickerson, I need that warrant. The animal hair, the human blood, the artifacts in Wilson's office and the names on the list are all connected somehow. I don't know how yet, but I intend to find out and I need the addresses of the young men on that list."

"That's pretty damn slim, Jack. I don't know if any

Judge will issue a warrant on just that. We have a slim chance with Judge Wilder. He is generally lenient. I'll approach him tomorrow, okay?"

"Okay, but please push it. I've got a feeling there is something going on with Wilson and Los Lobos."

Dickerson replied, "I'll see what I can do."

It was getting late in the afternoon when I walked in the Ironton Police Station. The desk Sergeant had to get a few ribs in at my expense. "Hey Jack, seen any more wolf men?"

"Nah, other than the one I'm looking at right now. It looks like your ears are getting pointy and is that hair I see growing on your knuckles?"

With that remark, he did his best imitation of a wolf howl.

"Damn Sarge, that sounds just like the howl I heard the other night. I might have to put you on my list of suspects."

Everyone around the desk started laughing. Soon Sarge and I joined in.

"Is Sanchez in?" I asked."

"Yeah Jack," he said between guffaws, "Go on back."

I still heard the laughter as I walked down the hall to Juan's office. Sticking my head in Juan's open door, I asked, "Juan, you got a minute?"

"Yeah Jack, come on in. What can I do for you?"

After explaining everything to Juan, I asked him to look over the list to see if he knew any of the young men. After studying it for a few minutes, he said, "I know five of the twelve. The top two, Eddie Crane and Tim Ebbert, have been in and out of trouble for several years. Eddie's Dad is the type that thinks his kid never does anything wrong. The few times I've had Eddie in here, his Dad said he was just mischievous. I told him Eddie was headed for big trouble if he didn't straighten him out. You want to hear what he said?"

"Yeah."

"Boys will be boys."

"What does Eddie's Mother say about him?"

"She died about fifteen years ago."

Do you know where the top two live?"

"Yeah, Eddie Crane lives on Sixth Street beside the funeral home and Tim Ebbert lives two doors down from Eddie."

"Well Juan, I'm going to pay a visit to these two young men. Want to come along?"

"No can do, Jack. I have to take my kid to football practice."

"Okay, I'll let you know the outcome of the meetings."

Driving up to Crane's house, I figured I'd have to be careful how I approached him, especially with Eddie's Dad being overly protective. I pulled up in front of the Crane house around 6:00 o'clock. Eddie's Dad answered the door and after I introduced my self, he invited me in. "Is Eddie in?" I asked.

Mr. Crane turned towards the stairs and yelled, "Eddie,

get your ass down here." Then turning back to me he asked, "Is he in trouble again?"

"No, it's nothing like that. I'm investigating the death of a counselor at the youth center and I need to ask Eddie a couple of questions."

Eddie came down the stairs and walked up to me with a swagger. "Yeah, what do you want?"

"Eddie, I'm Jack Stevens and I'm investigating the murder of Darrel Wilson. Did you know him?"

"Yeah."

"How did you know him, Eddie?"

"He was my counselor at the youth center."

"How long have you been going to the youth center?"

"A couple of years," he replied.

"How old are you Eddie?"

'Eighteen."

"When did you meet Mr. Wilson?"

"About a year ago, Why?"

"I told you. I'm investigating his death. Do you know of anyone who would want Mr. Wilson dead?"

"Nope, is that all?"

"No, I have one more question. What is Los Lobos?"

Eddie was cool but not cool enough to hide the surprise showing in his eyes.

He hesitated before he replied, "I don't know. You got anymore questions?"

"No, that's all for now. Thank you."

"Whatever," he replied.

After thanking Mr. Crane, I left and walked down two doors to Tim Ebbert's house.

I knocked on the door and Mrs. Ebbert, a widow, answered the door. Mrs. Ebbert invited me in and called Tim to the living room. I told him who I was and what I was doing. When I asked Tim the same questions, he had the same smug attitude as Eddie. When I mentioned Los Lobos, Tim's surprise was even more pronounced than Eddie's. These two kids knew something and I needed to get them away from their parents to grill them.

Chapter 6

Dickerson was unable to get a search warrant for the records at the youth center. My plan was to wait outside the youth center and watch for Eddie and Tim to show up. The following Friday night, I got lucky. Tim and Eddie showed up around 9:00 PM. I went in a few minutes after they went in and found them shooting a basketball on a makeshift basketball court. When they saw me, they quit playing. I walked up and took the ball away from Tim and shot a few baskets myself.

Eddie popped up, “You can’t come in here and do that.”

Tim looked kind of nervous when I said, “You don’t mind, do you Tim? Eddie and I are going to play a little one on one.”

“No,” he stammered, “Go ahead.”

I threw the ball to Eddie, “You take it out first, tough guy.”

Eddie came down the court, dribbling like a pro and when he got near me, I stuck out my foot and tripped him. Picking up the ball, I dribbled over to the basket and made the shot. Eddie got up, cursing like a sailor, “You can’t do that, it’s illegal.”

"Yes I can, Eddie. You're playing with the big boys now." I tossed the ball to him, "Your turn again, Eddie."

Eddie was mad as hell and threw the ball back to me as hard as he could. After catching it, I tossed it back with as much force as I could muster. Eddie wasn't ready and the ball hit him square in the nose. Blood was sprayed all over the floor.

"Well, Eddie, since you're injured, I guess Tim has to come in as substitute."

Tim was not real happy about that and was quick to say so, "I don't want to play."

"That's too bad, Tim. Both of you guys are into some real heavy crap. Both of you are involved in Los Lobos and I'm going to prove it. Eddie, you're eighteen and Tim you'll be eighteen in a few more months. You guys are entering adulthood and you're going to start paying adult prices for your actions. See you soon, men."

Eddie barked out, "Screw you, Stevens."

I turned and looked back at him, "Okay tough guy, you'll be the first to fall."

I left the youth center and headed back to my apartment. Around midnight, I heard a noise out on the stoop. Jumping out of bed, I grabbed my pistol and headed to the front door. When I snapped on the outside light, I saw a wolf's head starring at me through the window. As I reached for the door knob, the dammed thing took off down the stairs to the alley. When I stepped out on the landing, it stopped at the bottom of the stairs and let out an eerie howl. As I started off the landing, to go after it, I stumbled over something at me feet. Regaining my balance, I looked down to see a dead possum with its throat ripped out. Evidently, it was a warning from Los Lobos. It really pissed me off that an innocent animal had to die for their silly game. The rest of the night was spent waiting for that thing to come back.

Saturday morning, I called Sanchez and Dickerson and told them what happened and what my plans were. "I'm going to lean on Ebbert. He's cocky, but I think he'll crack if I push him hard enough. Sanchez, can you pick him up?"

"What kind of a charge can I use to pick him up?"

"Hell, I don't know, just pick him up. Suspicion of murder will allow us to hold him for a few hours."

"That's a pretty heavy charge, Jack."

"I know, but it's not going on his record, yet. Hell, get him on vandalism or anything, just to get him in here."

Dickerson spoke up, "Jack, are you sure you know what you're doing?"

"Yeah, I do," I replied.

Tim was picked up and brought in around 2:00 PM. His mother came with him and I had to smooth it over with her. I told her all we wanted to do was ask him some questions about Mr. Wilson. Tim was scared to death. He was trembling and just about ready to cry. "Tim, do you want an attorney present while we talk to you? You're entitled to one and if your Mother can't afford one, we can get a court appointed attorney."

Mrs. Ebbert spoke up and said, "We don't want or need an attorney. Tim, if these gentlemen ask you a question, I want you to tell the truth. Do you understand?"

"Yes Ma'am," Tim replied.

I started with the same basic questions I asked Tim before. When I got to the Los Lobos question, Tim hesitated.

"Timothy, answer the man," his Mother said.

I re-asked the question and he still hesitated to answer.

"Tim, I know you and Eddie were members of the club. I found a list of all the members and as we speak, the police are tracking down the others and they will be brought in for questioning. What did you do as a member of Los Lobos?"

Tim would not answer until his Mother smacked him on the back of the head and said, "Answer the man, Timothy."

Tim was sobbing uncontrollably and replied, "We acted like a pack of wolves."

"Where did that happen, Tim, at the youth center?"

"No," he managed to squeak out between sobs.

"Where Tim, tell me where you did this?"

"In a vacant building on Second Street."

"How did you act like wolves?"

"We had a wolf's head and skin that Mr. Wilson gave us. Someone would wear it and growl and act like a wolf."

"Who would that someone be, Tim?"

"Mostly, it was Eddie."

"Did Eddie have it on last night when he came to my door?"

"Yes."

"Did Eddie have it on a couple of weeks ago when I was in that building?"

"Yes."

"Who killed Mr. Wilson?"

"Eddie."

"When?"

"Mr. Wilson was killed a couple of days before and Eddie was going back to the building to drag him over to the railroad tracks."

"Why did he kill Mr. Wilson?"

"I don't know. Mr. Wilson was part of the club. He and Eddie started the club."

"Did Eddie stab Mr. Wilson by himself or were there other people involved?"

"I think they had an argument. Eddie said he had to kill Mr. Wilson because Mr. Wilson found out that Eddie shot a woman out on Ox Road. Eddie told me he liked killing so much, that after he killed a bum, he went out and shot that woman on Ox Road."

"Where did he get the gun?"

"It was his Fathers."

"What kind of gun was it?"

"A 38 snub nose pistol."

"What did Eddie do with the gun?"

"He said he buried it in the woods."

"Where?"

"Someplace on Ox Road."

"Tim, this question is important. Why did Eddie put nickels on the eyes of people he killed?"

"He read about the person strangling people and thought it would be cool to copy him."

"Okay Tim, I have one more question."

"What's that?"

"Were you ever involved in any of the killings?"

Tim replied "No," emphatically. "I swear to God I had nothing to do with any of them. I wasn't even around when Eddie did it. Eddie told me about them later."

"Right now, I believe you, but you're still in a lot of trouble. You withheld information that could have saved, at least, one person's life.

"I was scared; Eddie said he would kill me and my Mother."

"We'll take that into consideration, but you have to convince a Judge of that fact. It's not going to be easy because you've been in trouble before."

"I know, but I swear to God, I'm telling the truth."

"I have one more question, Tim. Do you know why the club was formed in the first place?"

"I don't know. Mr. Wilson and Eddie started the club."

I left Tim sitting in the interrogation room and took Mrs. Ebbert out in the hallway.

"Mrs. Ebbert, you know we're going to have to hold Tim for awhile. Until we pick up Eddie, I think you should stay here also. We have a room that we use to hold people to keep them safe. It has a couple of cots in it. At least, you'll be able to sleep safely."

"Thank you Mr. Stevens, I may have to spend the night, but I don't think I'll be sleeping much."

"As soon as we get Eddie, you can return home. Right now, it's safer if you stay here."

I called Juan down to the interrogation room and he witnessed Tim's statement to a court stenographer. With that out of the way, a warrant was issue for Eddie Crane. At 7:15 PM, the warrant was placed in my hand and Juan told me,

"Go get him."

At 7:30 PM, I pulled up in front of the Crane house. Mr. Crane saw me pull up and came out of the house to meet me. "Mr. Crane, do you know where Eddie is?"

"He left about fifteen minutes ago."

"Do you know where he went?"

"Why?" he replied.

"I have a couple more questions to ask him."

"Damn, don't you people ever give up?"

"I'm sorry you feel that way. We are just trying to be thorough. A person died a horrible death and we are just trying to find out why. We would do the same investigation for you."

With disgust, Mr. Crane replied, "Eddie said he was going to the youth center. Go ask him your damn questions, then leave him alone."

"Yes sir, thank you. Oh, by the way, do you own a pistol?"

"Not any more, someone stole it about six months ago."

"What kind was it?"

"A 38 snub nose revolver."

"Did you report it stolen?"

"Nah, it wasn't worth much, why?"

"We found one a while back and I ask everyone I talk to the same question."

After leaving the Crane household, I headed for the youth center. When I walked in, Eddie was no where to be seen. I asked a group of kids standing off to the side, "You guys seen Eddie Crane tonight?"

A young man replied, "He went up the street to get something to eat, said he be back later."

There was nothing left for me to do but go back outside and wait. About a half hour later, I saw Eddie pull up and get out of his car. When I jumped out of my car and started for him, he saw me and sprinted back towards his vehicle. I grabbed him just as he was ready to open the door. Eddie broke loose and took a swing at me. When I saw it coming, I caught a glimpse of steel in his right hand. That punk was trying to cut me. I jumped back far enough that I didn't get the full brunt of the blade. Still, the blade caused a nasty scratch from my ear to my chin. Eddie was insane. As he drew back for another swing at me, I was able to jump in, grab his hand and smash it on the hood of the car. After I smashed his hand the third time, the knife clattered down the hood. Eddie was putting up a good struggle until I popped him three times in the head. After Eddie collapsed in a heap, I rolled him over and put my knee on his neck. Grabbing his flailing arms, I managed to get the cuffs on him. In the melee, Eddie's left shirt sleeve was torn revealing a bandage on his left bicep. "What happened Eddie, gunshot?"

"Screw you, Stevens."

I wanted so much to stomp the hell out of him, but I couldn't. Being a legitimate cop, I had to follow the law. But what the hell, I gave him a swift kick in the ribs, left him lying in the street and walked over to my car and to call in.

"Sarge, tell Sanchez to come get this punk before I kill him."

"Where are you, Jack?"

"At the youth center."

"Okay, stay cool. We'll be there in a few minutes. Just stay cool."

When I walked back to Eddie, he was trying to get up. "Stay down, Eddie. You're going to get hurt."

Eddie was screaming like a mad man, "Let me up, I'll kill you."

"I don't think so," I replied, as I pushed him back down in the street and slapped another set of cuffs on his ankles. In about three minutes, I heard the Ironton Police sirens screaming. Eddie was still yelling as the police hauled him away. Eddie was going to trial for three brutal murders; Darrell Wilson, Marie Iverson and John Doe. In my opinion, he should receive the death penalty, but I was not the judge and jury. Later at the trial, Tim was sentenced to six months in a juvenile detention home and placed on five years probation, as were the rest of the Los Lobos members. The wolf suit was found at Eddie's house, hidden in the attic. When the wolf suit was presented as evidence at the trial, Eddie stood and howled. It took three bailiffs to remove him from the court room. When the howl echoed through the courtroom, it sent chills up my spine. Eddie was sentenced to the rest of his natural life in an institution for the criminally insane. That wrapped up three of the murders, Iverson, John Doe, and Wilson. While the case was solved, I still had a question. Why was Los Lobos formed? I would dig into that later. Right now, I had another madman to find.

Who was responsible for the murders of Jennings and Hannon?

Monday after the trial, I told Dickerson, I needed some time alone.

"Where you going," he asked?

"I think I'll go out to Lake Vesuvius and drown a few worms. It's been a long time since I've sat on a shore and thought about absolutely nothing."

After I threw a bed roll on the beast, tied some fishing gear on and headed out to the lake. At the lake, I threw everything in a rented canoe and paddled out in the lake. Since there were already several fishermen in the process of dunking their lines, I paddled on past them. I didn't want to be around other people. The place I wanted was near the headwaters of the lake. Once past the main body of the lake, the water was calm and serene. Every now and then, I'd see a ripple in the water ahead of me. The fish were filling their bellies with water skaters. I don't know the name of the bugs they were picking off, but I always called them water skaters as they looked like they were skating on the water. As I got closer to the headwaters of the lake, the lake became shallow and narrow. Soon, there wasn't enough room to turn the canoe around. I beached it and drug it up on the shore. Retrieving my fishing gear, it was just a matter of minutes until I caught a nice trout. After I cleaned it, I built a fire, wrapped it in foil and leaned back to wait.

Darkness was starting to envelope the woods and soon the stars were plainly visible. They looked like diamonds sparkling on black velvet. While never being a stargazer, I was able to pick out the Big Dipper. The filets were still sizzling on the fire when I snatched then out. After eating the best meal I'd had in long time, I leaned the canoe on its side, opened the bed roll and lay down for a little snooze.

The next morning, I awoke refreshed and ready to explore. After dousing the embers in the fire pit, I struck out for parts unknown. Every now and then, I'd turn around to see what it looked like behind me. I'd heard too many stories about people getting lost in the woods because they did not stop and look where they came from.

If you don't know where you came from, you can't reasonably expect to get back to your starting point. Wild berries and nuts were my breakfast and lunch. After six hours of roaming through the woods, I started back to my campsite. When I came out of a patch of woods, I encountered a creek. Evidently, I made a wrong turn. Now I knew why my name was Jack Stevens instead of Daniel Boone. I threw a few leaves in the slow moving water to see which way was down stream. About three hours later, I was back at my campsite loading my gear in the canoe. Around 7:00 PM, I was back at the rental place stashing my gear back on the beast.

Chapter 7

When I reported in on Wednesday, I was surprised to learn the strangler had claimed another victim. Dickerson told me it happened Monday night around 11:00 o'clock on Railroad Street in an old abandoned building. The victim was a hobo everyone called Uncle Charlie. He did odd jobs around town and when the weather started turning cold, he took off south to warmer temperatures, to return in the spring each year. Charlie was a man in his early sixties and had been around town about fifteen years. As in the other two unsolved cases, nickels were found on Charlie's eyes. His murder was really sad because Charlie was a happy go lucky individual. As long as he had a few bucks for beer and cigarettes, he was happy. His normal routine was to tie one on, sober up in a few days, get another odd job and earn enough money for more booze. Before my Father died, he would let Charlie cut the grass every now and then. It was ironic that Charlie was selected as a victim, he would have been moving on in a few weeks.

I told Dickerson, "I'm going over the coroner's office to see the body and see what George has to say."

"Okay Jack, let me know if you find out anything."

"Will do."

George Young, the County Coroner, had his office in the basement of the Sheriff's building. "Hey George. How are you doing?"

"I'm fine Jack, how about you?"

"Okay, I just came over to see what you had on Uncle Charlie.

"Come back here with me, Jack. I want to show you something."

We walked into the morgue and George walked up to a drawer and pulled it out far enough to expose Charlie's upper body. When he pulled the sheet back, he said, "Look at the bruises on his neck."

As I leaned closer, I asked, "What's so special about them?"

"Come on Jack, look how big they are."

George was no small man and when he placed his hands around Charlie's neck the bruises were much bigger than his hand.

"Damn George, the bastard that did this must be huge."

"I don't know about that, Jack, but he certainly has huge hands."

"George, did the bruises on the other two victims match Charlie's?"

"Yes," he replied.

It was time to pay another visit to Mr. Adams. I found him at the gas station and the first thing I asked him was,

"Where were you Monday between the hours of 6:00 PM and midnight?"

"Why" he replied?

"Don't get cute with me. I asked you a question and if I don't get a straight answer, I'll cave in your face. Now answer the damn question."

"Okay," he replied, "Don't get your dander up. I was here working."

"Yeah right, I guess you worked until midnight."

"As a matter of fact, I worked until 2:00 AM Tuesday morning."

"Can you prove that?"

"Yeah, just ask my boss. He was here with me. We had a rush job on a transmission."

"Where is he?"

"He went to pick up lunch, should be back in a few minutes."

His boss showed up in about fifteen minutes and confirmed Adams was with him during that time period.

On the way back to Ironton, I kept wondering about a connection to these three deaths. We had to come up with a connection if we ever expected to solve the deaths of these three men. When I arrived at the office I learned that arrangements were being made to bury Charlie in a pauper's grave at the local cemetery. I had to come up with a connection, for these three men, Alan Jennings, William Hannon, and Uncle Charlie. Jennings was from Ironton. Hannon was from Coal Grove, and Uncle Charlie was from wherever. I studied the cases until it was time to go home. Lying awake that night, I agonized over the deaths, but no amount of agonizing would give me any clues as to a common denominator. What was I missing? I visited Mrs. Jennings and Mrs. Hannon to see if they had ever heard of Uncle Charlie. Neither one was familiar with him.

The nickels on the eyes were the most baffling. Why did the killer do that? What was the meaning of the nickels? I'd lay awake at night trying to fathom a reason. If I couldn't make a connection, it would present a scenario that was especially frightening, a killer that killed just for the thrill of it.

The Friday after Charlie's body was found, I visited the crime scene. The murder had taken place only a couple of blocks from the police station. When I walked in the abandoned building, there were four hobos sitting on the floor. "Hey guys, how are you doing?" No one spoke so I told them who I was. "I'm Jack Stevens, Federal Agent I'm investigating Charlie's death." When I said Federal Agent, all four got up real quick and started to leave. "Hold it guys, I'm not here to hassle you. I just want to ask you a few questions. After I get finished, you can get back to whatever you do." All four of them returned to a squatting position around a small fire burning in a lard can.

"Okay mister, what do you want to know?"

"How long have you guys been coming around here?"

The speaker appeared to be a guy in his early sixties and seemed to be the leader. He told me, "We've been here about four months. We stay until it gets cold and then we head south."

"Were any of you guys around when Charlie got killed?"

The room got real quite and I thought maybe it was too soon to ask that question. "Forget that for a minute. What do you guys do for food?"

The leader spoke again, "Sometimes we get lucky and pick up a job here and there. You know, cutting grass, washing windows or maybe sweeping up. We do most anything for a few bucks."

"What if there aren't any odd jobs around?"

"Sometimes, we panhandle and sometimes we check out the dumpsters behind restaurants. You gotta do what you gotta do to eat."

"Listen guys, there's a church up the street that gives free meals a couple of times a week."

"Yeah, we know. Sometimes, we go up there. Once or twice they let us sleep in the basement of the church."

Sensing it was time to ask the question, I looked the leader square in the eye and asked, "Were you here the night Charlie got killed?"

Hesitantly, he answered, "Yes."

"Tell me what happened?"

"I heard someone come in and I thought it was the cops coming in to hassle us. You know they do that a couple of times a week. Earl and Jim took off out a back window. Me and Frank tried to wake up Charlie, but he had a few drinks that night and he was slow to get moving. Me and

Frank took off as Charlie was getting up and we waited out back for Charlie to come out. When He didn't, I sneaked back in looking for him. When I came around this corner, right here, I saw Charlie on the floor with a man kneeling next to him. The man had his hands around Charlie's throat and Charlie wasn't making any noise or struggling. I figured he was dead and sneaked back out."

"Did you see the man's face?"

"Nah, his head was turned away from me."

"What was he wearing?"

"Dark pants and a dark shirt."

"How about his hair, was it long or short?"

"Short, it kind of looked like it was cut like a flat top."

"Could you tell what color it was?"

"Well it was dark in here but it looked like it was light. You know, white or blond."

"Did you go around to the front after you went out of the building?"

"Yeah, I did."

"What did you see?"

"I saw that guy walking down the street."

"Did you see a car?"

"Yeah."

"Did you get a license number?"

"Nah, all I saw was an S on the tag."

"Do you know what kind of car it was?"

"It kind of looked like a Chevy. It didn't look new, maybe a year or two old and a dark color."

"How tall do you think he was?"

"His car was parked close to a telephone pole. He stopped for a second and looked up and down the street, got in his car and took off. When he stood there for a second, he looked about three feet short of the climbing spikes on the pole."

"Will you show me which pole it was?"

We walked down the street and he pointed out the pole. The spikes were a little over eight feet from the ground. I figured the killer to be about five feet six inches tall. Probably someone with the short man syndrome

I thanked him and told him he had been a big help. I gave him thirty bucks and told him, "Go get you guys something to eat and don't spend it all on booze, okay?"

He thanked me and headed back down the street. I stood there a few minutes and soon all four men come out of the building. When they walked by me, one of them said,

"Thanks, Mister."

"You're welcome guys."

I walked on back to the station and Dickerson just happened to be coming out.

"Come on back in with me, Dickerson, we need to talk to Juan."

"Okay Jack, what you got?"

"I have some info on Charlie's killer."

We walked to Juan's office and I started telling them what I found out. "Small man, about 5'6", light colored hair, maybe a flat top or cut close, drives a late model Chevy, dark in color, has a tag that starts in S.

"Can't be more than a couple thousand like that," replied Juan.

"Damn Juan, it's more than we had."

"I know Jack; I'm not putting you down. I'm just frustrated by the case, especially since Charlie was killed just a few blocks from the station."

"Listen guys, my own personal opinion is that these three murders are the work of a deranged person. None of the victims had anything in common and I think he picks his victims at random."

"You may be right, Jack. Where does that leave us?"

"With one incredibly hard job. I think we need to tell our local cops to be on the look out for any late model dark Chevy's, especially if a light haired person is driving it." After we talked a while longer, I decided to go home.

Sleep came slowly that night but I had the satisfaction that we were a little closer to the killer than we were a couple of weeks ago. That night was when the nightmares began. I dreamed I was walking along Railroad Street and I saw a dark figure stalking someone. After a couple of blocks, he fixated on a lone figure by a darkened alley. Running towards them, I hoped to get there in time to stop the murder. When I got within a few feet, he turned towards me. His face was shrouded in a fog and an eerie laughter came from within the fog. His hands wrapped around my throat and started squeezing the life out of me.

I couldn't breathe and was losing consciousness. As quickly as he appeared, he vanished into thin air but I could still hear the eerie laughter. I frantically turned around, but he was nowhere in sight. As the laughter faded out, I was left standing in a cloud of fog. When the wind swirled the fog away, I was standing in the middle of an unfamiliar road. On my left was a lane leading through a patch of woods. I had an uncontrollable urge to start walking that lane and it led to an old Victorian house in the middle of a clearing. The doors and windows were covered with plywood and the overgrown yard was bathed in moonlight. As I stood at the edge of the yard, diaphanous human forms appeared to rise from the yard and their open mouthed moans seemed to be inviting me to enter. I took the first few steps towards them and when I reached for the wrought iron gate, I awoke in my bed. My body was drenched with sweat and I was shivering uncontrollably. In my mind, I could still see the house. There was something evil inside that house. What, I didn't know.

I got out of bed, turned on the lights and sat at my kitchen table, with pistol in hand. Around 6:00 AM, I went to shave and stood there shaking. In the mirror, I saw bruises on my neck. I knew I had to find that house. I knew it existed, but where?

When I got to work, I told Dickerson about my dream.

"Jack, you've gone off the deep end. Are you nuts?"

"Dickerson, I don't know what the hell is going on. That

dream was as real to me as you sitting there. If I'm nuts, please explain these bruises on my neck?"

Dickerson sat there for a couple of seconds before he spoke, "Jack, you're in this thing way to deep. You need to take a few days off. Come back to work when you got your head screwed on straight."

"I'm okay, it was just a nightmare.'

"Jack, I mean it. You're a good cop and I don't want you freaking out on me. Take the time off. That's an order."

"Okay," I replied.

I went back home and after I packed some clothes, I straddled the beast and headed for Columbus, Ohio. Family was a major need of mine at this time. I don't want to say, I was going to see my Mommy, but that was exactly what I was going to do. It was late afternoon when I pulled in Mom's driveway. Aunt Charlene was out sweeping the front porch. When she saw me pull up she stuck her head in the door and hollered,

"Sis, that big lug is back and I think he needs another hug."

Little did she know that was exactly what I needed. Mom came out and passed out a couple of big hugs and I felt a little better. She had supper cooking on the stove and all three of us went in and had a good supper. After supper, I finally got around to telling Mom about my dream. Mom surprised me when she said,

"Jack, I think I've seen that house, too. I don't know where, but it sure sounds familiar.

"Did you see it in a dream, Mom?"

"I don't know son, I just don't know. Maybe I've actually seen it."

"Where, Mom. Try to remember. It's very important."

"I'll try, Jack. If I remember, I'll let you know."

"Okay, now let's quit talking about it. The whole thing gives me the willies."

I went to bed and got the first full night's sleep in several months, no dreams or nightmares. After arising the next morning, I told Mom, "I'm going over to the cemetery in Gahanna."

"Why, she replied?

I told her about Barbara and how I felt about her. "Mom, I have one other thing to tell you."

"What's that," she replied?

"You may think I'm crazy, but sometimes I hear her voice. It's like she's my guardian angel. In fact she came to me in a vision one time a while back. I'm not crazy, am I?"

"No Jack, you're not crazy. I believe in guardian angels, also. Sometimes, I feel as though you father is talking to me."

"Whew, I thought I was cuckoo."

"No darling, you're not cuckoo. One thing you're forgetting is your heritage. Your Great Great Grandmother was a full blooded Cherokee and the wife of a powerful Tribal Medicine man. One thing I never told you boys about, your Father had visions when he was younger. Maybe your Father's gift was passed on to you."

"Mom, did any of my brothers have the gift?"

"I don't think so," she replied, "if they did, they never said anything to me about it."

"Thanks for sharing that with me, Mom, I feel much better."

I gave Mom a hug and rode over to the cemetery in Gahanna. Sitting on the ground by Barbara's grave, I talked to her just like she was sitting beside me. Most of the afternoon passed before I realized it. I placed a kiss on my finger tips and touched Barbara's grave and when I rose to leave, I heard Barbara's voice, "The house is real. Be careful, it is full of evil."

I smiled as serene feeling spread through me.

I headed back to Mom's and spent the next four days there. We had a great time. When we weren't shopping, we were eating. We talked to the wee hours of the morning and usually got up around noon every day. I told Mom and Aunt Charlene it was the best time I had in months. Friday, I said my good-byes and headed back to Ironton. When I got home in the late afternoon, I decided it was time to spend a day or two with my brother since I didn't have to be back to work until Monday.

Jerry and I went fishing on the Ohio River. I guess I'd better clarify that statement. It was more like drowning worms. We caught a couple of catfish and threw them back in. It really didn't matter to me if we caught anything. We had a great time reliving childhood stories. One story in particular was about the Stevens boys always altering their bicycles. Since my father kept most of his tools in the car, the only thing we had to work with was a small pipe wrench. As everyone knows, if you use a pipe wrench on a nut or bolt, it will eventually chew it up and sharp edges will protrude from it. Jerry was riding a friend on the handle bars when the bicycle's front wheel stopped dead in a ditch. While the bike came to a dead stand still, Jerry's friend kept going forward. He ripped his pants, plus a big chunk out of his rear end when he slid across the chewed up bolt. Jerry and I sat there laughing until we had tears in our eyes. It was hilarious to watch the friend jumping around in the middle of the road holding his rear end with both hands. We had an old saying back then, "Off with your head and a chunk out of your butt." Jerry's friend still had his head; he just lost a big chunk of his butt.

Later, I told Jerry about the house in the dream. The description meant nothing to him so I dropped it. Around 7:00 PM, we were headed back to Jerry's house when he suddenly slammed on the brakes. Looking up, I saw an apparition of the strangler standing in the middle of the lane. His face was shrouded in a fog.

"Do you see that?" asked Jerry.

"Yeah," I replied, "I've seen it a few times before."

"What the hell is it?"

"It's the person I'm looking for. It's as if he is taunting me. I don't know if it's from my mind or his, but I'm going to meet that bastard some day."

"What do we do now?" asked Jerry.

"Keep driving, hit him."

Jerry started inching forward.

"No Jerry, I said hit him."

Stretching my leg across the floorboard, I stepped on Jerry's foot. The motor revved and the car shot forward. As we hit the image, it dissolved, rolled back over the hood, and disappeared over the top of the car. Turning around to look out the back window, I saw nothing but fog as it dissipated in thin air. Jerry was visibly shaken and excitedly said.

"Jack, I don't know what you're into, but you better get the hell out of it."

"I can't, brother. That bastard has strangled three innocent people, plus God only knows how many more. This guy has to be stopped."

"I hope he don't get you, Jack." Jerry replied.

"Me too," I said.

Chapter 8

Sunday was uneventful, no visions or nightmares. When I reported for work on Monday, Dickerson asked, "Your head back on straight?"

"Yeah, I'm okay."

"Have you had any more visions or nightmares?"

"Nah, everything is copasetic."

"Good, I was beginning to worry about you."

"I'm fine Dickerson. Do you need me for anything in particular today?"

"No, Why?"

"I've got a hunch and I need to check it out."

"Listen Jack, you're not going off on a wild goose chase, are you?"

"No Dickerson. I've just got a hunch and I want to check it out."

"Okay, Jack, just don't do anything stupid, okay?"

"Okay boss."

There was no way I was telling Dickerson I was searching for a haunted house. I took off and drove up and down every street in town. While I passed several houses that looked similar, none of them was the one I was looking for. I wanted a two and a half story Victorian, dark gray in color, dark shutters, and a wrought iron fence that surrounded the yard. There would be evil eyed gargoyles staring down from the corners of the roof. It was a long shot that did not pan out. I knew the house was somewhere; I'd just have to expand my search to find it. If Dickerson knew I was searching for a haunted house, he would think I've lost my mind and have me removed from the force. That house and the strangler had to be connected somehow.

I needed an ally. After going through several possibilities, I settled on Don Hamilton. I called Don at home that evening. "Hey Don, this is Jack. Man, I need to talk to you, but it has to remain confidential. Do you think you can come to my apartment on Saturday or Sunday?"

"Sure Jack, what's it about?"

"I know it sounds strange, but I really need your help with something and I can't tell you until we're face to face. Do you think you can make it this weekend?"

"Okay Jack. Since we were partners, I'll see you around 10:00 o'clock Saturday morning. That time okay?"

"Yes, and thanks Don."

Ten o'clock, Saturday morning, Don came knocking on my door. "Good morning, Don, How are you?"

"I don't know yet. I guess it depends on what you got to say."

"I got some fresh coffee on the stove, you want a cup?"

"Yeah, a little cream, no sugar."

We sat down at the kitchen table and I told Don everything from the murder of Uncle Charlie, the visions of the house, and about the vision at the river bank. Don sat there for a minute before he spoke.

"That's a lot to digest at one time, Jack. I don't mean to be a smart ass, but have you seen a Doctor?"

"Do you mean a shrink?" I replied.

"Well... Yeah. What you just told me was some pretty strange shit."

"I know it's strange, Don, but I'm not crazy."

"Dammit Jack, I never said you was crazy."

"Hell Don, there were times when I thought I was. I talked to my mother last week and I even asked her if I was cuckoo. She told me no and then told me to remember my heritage. My Great Great Grandmother was a full blooded Cherokee and the wife of a Tribal Medicine Man. The last thing she told me was about my Father. He also had visions. She never told us as little children because she did not know it the gift had been passed on. I don't know why the gift was passed on to me, but I'm not going to ignore it. I know the whole police force is on the look out for a dark Chevy driven by a light haired person. What I need, is if you or the guys see one, don't stop it. Instead, give me a call on the radio or at home depending on the time of day or night. Let me know where you are so I can follow the car. I can be anywhere in town in just a matter of minutes. The person that drives that car is an evil bastard. He's already killed three people and I fear there's more around that house I dream about. If you stop him, we may never know if there are other victims."

"Is that it," Don asked as he breathed a sigh of relief, "I thought you were going to ask me to kill somebody."

"Yeah, that's it."

"I can do that, Jack. I'll make sure the other cops know about it and call you. This will be between us and the patrolmen."

"Thanks Don, I felt I could count on you."

The days passed like molasses in January. Occasionally, I'd get a call from Don or one of the other police officers. "Jack, there's a late model Chevy going south on Third Street, 800 block, light haired individual." I'd run out to the beast, jump on and take off for South Third Street. When I got near the police tailing the car, I'd flash my headlight and fall in behind them. They would break off the tail and I'd follow the vehicle to its destination and usually it was a false trail. One time in particular, I followed a car, being driven by a white haired person of short stature, from North Fifth Street out to Ox Road. Dead smack in the middle of the road, the car stopped and a little old white haired lady jumped out and trotted back to my bike stuck a pistol in my ear and demanded to know why I was following her. "Take it easy Ma'am, I'm a cop."

"Let me see some ID." she demanded.

I complied and told her that I saw she was traveling alone and I just wanted to make sure she got home safe.

"I appreciate that sonny, but as you can see, I can take care of myself."

"Yes Ma'am, but please put that gun away before someone gets hurt. I'd also be careful who I pulled it on. Someone else might not be as understanding as I am."

I turned the beast around and headed back to my apartment. I lay down and tried to get some sleep, which was elusive. While I did manage to catch a few winks, that house kept popping up in my dreams.

That house was ominous looking in my dreams. The moon was playing peek-a-boo behind the clouds and the ground was heavy with a mist. From the mist, I saw the same apparitions emerge. There were black holes where their eyes would have been and their mouths were open as if screaming or gasping for breath. Their moans and screams were rolling around inside my head. I had to find out what was inside that house. My hands trembled as I approached the gate. When the latch handle snapped open, it sounded like an explosion in my head. As I swung the gate open, I expected a long squeak from the rusty hinges, but what I heard was an eerie sounding moan. It was as if the gate was a living thing. After a few steps up the sidewalk, I heard the gate swing shut. I did not turn around as I could not take my eyes off the house. As I got closer to the house, the apparitions returned to the mist.

When I stepped up on the porch, the creaking of the boards was amplified in my head. There was a number over the front door and as I rubbed the years of grime from it, the number 999 appeared. Finding the front door boarded up and impenetrable, I looked to my right and discovered an edge of a board covering a window was loose. After much pulling and tugging, I was able to remove about half of the board. Peeking in the window almost caused my heart to explode. Standing there, his face shrouded in fog, was the strangler. As I stood rooted in fear, the shroud evaporated to reveal a face with nickels on his eyes. Huge hands came through the glass, encircled my throat and squeezed until I was gasping for every breath I drew. The power in those hands was frightening as I felt my windpipe collapse. I was losing consciousness.

I awoke screaming. My throat hurt and I was gasping for breath. Laying there, drenched in sweat, my chest was heaving as I sucked in as much air as I could. After my heart returned to normal and my breathing was regular, I went into the kitchen... It was only an hour or so until it was time to get up for work. After putting on a pot of coffee, I sat there until daybreak.

I reported for work around 10:00AM and told Dickerson, "I want a copy of all the missing person reports for the last two years."

"Damn it Jack, that will amount to quite a few if you include Kentucky and West Virginia."

"Then make it a list of all missing within a fifty mile radius of Ironton, to include Kentucky and West Virginia."

"Okay Jack, it'll take a few days to get the information from the state agencies."

"I don't care, just do it."

"Jack, are you on to something?"

"Right now, I don't know. We're not making much headway with the strangler and maybe I'm just grabbing at straws."

Since it would be several days before the information was ready, I was assigned a bank robbery that just happened an hour ago. The robber was not real bright. He entered the bank about ten minutes before he robbed it. The bank teller said he came in to cash a check and when she asked him for identification he said he left it in his car. When he came back in to rob the bank, he forgot a couple of things. Number one was that his name, Dave, was on the left breast pocket and the other was the company he worked for was embroidered on the back of his jacket. That was about as good a clue as you could get, unless the jacket belonged to someone else. I took the information and drove out to Chisholm Tire in Franklin Furnace. I walked in and saw a young guy that matched the description of Dave. In fact, his name was embroidered on the breast pocket. "Hi Dave."

"Hi," he replied, "who are you?"

"I'm Jack, you ready to go?"

"Go where?" he asked

"To jail," I replied as I snapped the cuffs on him.

When I searched his pockets, he had over four thousand dollars in his front pocket. His boss, Ed Chisholm came running out of his office to see what was going on.

"Well, Ed, young Dave robbed the bank on his way to work this morning.

Ed spoke up, "Dave, you told me you were going to the doctor this morning. You robbed the bank? That was a stupid thing to do."

"You know Ed, he's so stupid, I really hate to arrest him, but he did break the law. Come on Dave, let's go."

The second case was an armed robbery on Second Street. I swung by the Ironton Police department to find out the status on the case. When I walked in the police station, Charlie Simpson, a local cop, started howling. I would have to put up with that for the rest of my life. Maybe a better way of saying that, I would have to put up with that for the rest of his life. "Charlie, you know there are ten thousand comedians out of work, now there are ten thousand and one."

There were several cops in the squad room and Don Hamilton was standing off to one side. I walked up and asked him the status on the armed robbery.

"We solved that about a half hour ago. Turned out it was an ex-employee of the restaurant. The restaurant manager was on the way back from the bank with a bag full of change for the day. He recognized the robber's voice. We picked him up about a half hour later and he confessed." Those robberies were the only excitement for the week so I ended up doing patrol duties for the rest of the week. Drunks and speeders were all I encountered the rest of the week.

CHAPTER 9

Friday, before I left work, Dickerson came by my desk and plopped down a stack of folders. After thumbing through the files, sixteen in all, I told Dickerson,

"I'll take them home with me. I need something to do this weekend."

Fifteen missing persons and one file had a rap sheet of a person that used the same MO of strangulation. Unfortunately, for us, he was still serving time in the Summitt Correctional Facility. I left work and drove by the Big Boy Restaurant, ordered a carry out meal and headed to my apartment. After eating, I started reviewing the folders of the missing persons. Out of a total of fifteen, six were unaccounted for. Of the nine accounted for, six were living under an assumed name on the west coast. One was found in New York City and two were murdered, one in Los Angeles and one in Chicago. Of the six still missing, there were not any common threads. The ages ranged from twenty four to forty seven. There were four males and two females. As I studied the six missing person's reports, I kept looking for a common denominator. Six people just don't disappear off the face of the earth and not leave a trace somewhere. As a last resort, I dug out a map and placed pins in each of the missing person's home town. All six fell within a twenty mile circle, with Ironton being at the northern edge of the circle. We were looking for a local killer; maybe it was time to expand our search into Kentucky.

Monday, Dickerson and I drove over the Ohio River Bridge into Kentucky and rode out to the State Police Barracks on US 60. After we talked to Major J.R. Thompson, he promised the cooperation of the Kentucky State Police. "The only problem" he stated, "is that Jack will not be allowed to make arrests in the State and he will always have to have a Kentucky officer with him when he is in Kentucky."

"That's going to be a problem,' I replied, "I never know where I'm going to be at any given moment. Sometimes, I'm on an investigation twenty four hours a day."

Dickerson thanked Thompson for his time and told him we'd have to get back to him. "Before I do that, is there any chance Jack can get a special deputization to work in Kentucky?"

Thompson, replied, "I'll have to check on that."

Dickerson and I left and on the way back to Ohio, he told me, "I got the problem solved. I'll renew your special deputation as a Federal Agent. That way we don't need to wait on Thompson."

When I got back to my apartment that night, I started making notes on the missing victims.

Victim 1—Emily Watson, Age 27, Disappeared from Ashland, Kentucky, Registered Nurse at a local hospital Survived by husband and two boys, Reported missing 02/28/62, Husband suspected, Cleared 04/62

Victim 2—Jim Stone, Age 47, Bachelor, Missing 05/62 from Summit, Kentucky, No known relatives, Reported missing by neighbor, Unknown background

Victim 3—Jane Ulster, Age 31, Cannonsburg, Kentucky Reported missing by Mother, Mrs. J. Waugh, Jane was Divorced, No kids, husband remarried, Mother believes Ulster took off to start a new life, Disappeared 07/62

Victim 4—Raymond Strong, Age 45, Catlettsburg Kentucky, Fireman, Retired for Dept. service of 20 years, Single, Reported missing 04/63

Victim 5—Tom Castle, Age 45, Farmer, Missing Sybene, Ohio, Reported missing by Mother, Mother Co-owner of farm. Missing 05/63

Victim 6—Ed Hopkins, Age 39, Local businessman Hardware store, Chesapeake, Ohio, Survived by wife and one daughter. Reported missing 07/63

I realized my next step was to visit the relatives and

neighbors of the missing persons. I had to get more background on each of the individuals. I figured I might as well start in Ashland, Kentucky and work my way around the circle. In my heart, I had the feeling the missing persons were the victims of foul play.

Emily Watson was the first person on my list. When I knocked on the door at Watson's, a distinguished looking gentleman in his late thirties answered. "Mr. Watson, I'm Jack Stevens, a Federal Agent. I'm investigating your wife's disappearance. May I come in and talk to you for a while?"

"Come in, Mr. Stevens, what can I do to help?"

"I have a few questions, if you don't mind answering them? I know you've been through this before and I'll try to be brief."

"Ask all the questions you want," he replied, "I want to know what happened to her. It's been two years and I still miss her terribly. She was the love of my life."

"I'm sure she was a lovely woman."

"Thank you, Mr. Stevens."

"Please, call me Jack."

"Okay. What questions do you have?"

"She worked at a local hospital, correct?'

"Yes, she was working the evening shift and she had a Doctor's appointment before she was supposed to report in at 3:30. Around 3:15, she called and said she was at work and would be home around 11:30 or 12:00. I put the boys to bed around 8:00 o'clock and was watching television while I waited for her to come home. I fell asleep on the couch and woke up around 1:00 AM. I figured Emily went on to bed without waking me. Sometimes, because I don't sleep real well, she would let me sleep. After I woke up, I walked into the bedroom. She was not there and the bed covers weren't even turned down. I called the hospital and they told me she left about 11:15. It's only a half hour drive home and I got scared that she may have had car trouble. I bundled up the boys and went looking for her. When I couldn't find her, I was frantic. I called the police and when they couldn't find her, they tried to say that I had something to do with her disappearance. If the boys weren't with me, I'd whipped every one of them. About a week later, they found her car out on Centerline Road. It looked like a struggle had taken place inside the car. Emily was kind of short and had to use a cushion to sit on. The cushion was thrown over in the passenger side floor along with her purse, which had its contents strewn all over the floor. The police checked for finger prints on the car but all they could find were Emily's. Volunteers searched the area for a body, but everywhere they searched, they came up empty handed."

"Why did she go to the Doctor, that day?"

"She had a cold and wanted to get some medicine to make her feel better."

"What Doctor did she go to?"

"Doctor Robert Jenkins."

"Where is his office?"

"In Russell, Kentucky."

"Just a few more questions and I'll be out of your hair."

"You're not a problem, Jack. I'm willing to talk to anyone, anywhere, who might be able to find out what happened to Emily."

"Did she ever tell you about any trouble at work?"

"What do you mean," he replied?

"Was anyone bothering her at work?"

"Well... Yes, kind of. She mentioned something about an orderly giving her some kind of trouble. I asked her if she wanted me to talk to him and she said she could handle it. It's been so long but I think his name was Ron something or other."

"Other than the cold, did she have any thing else that may have affected her health?"

"No, she always said she was as healthy as a horse."

"One more question, Mr. Watson, and please bear with me. Would she run off with another man?"

"Hell no, we loved each other. We had two wonderful boys who were the apple of their Mother's eye. Emily was loved by me and the boys and in turn, she loved us."

"I didn't mean to offend you, but it was a question I had to ask. From what I've seen and heard, I felt the answer would be no. If you think of anything, no matter how trivial you think it is, please call me. I want to know what happened to Emily as much as you do."

I gave him my card and left.

While I believed Mr. Watson's story, I had to get

confirmation from the local police department. While I didn't get a warm reception, they did verify his story. As I left, I turned and told the Chief, "I know you don't like Feds coming in and nosing around, but keep one thing in mind. We are on the same team. All I'm trying to do is find out what happened to Emily Watson."

The hospital where Emily worked gave a glowing description of her. One of the nurses told me that Emily was all the time saying how happy she was and how much she loved her family. As I was getting ready to leave, one of the Nurses, M.J. Adams, told me, "Wait a minute, Mr. Stevens. I don't know if I should be saying this, but a few weeks before she disappeared that she told me she discovered a lump in her breast. She was supposed to have a biopsy a few days after she disappeared."

"Did she say if she thought it was cancer?"

"No. she just said she had a lump."

"Miss Adams, do you know if any of her family had cancer?"

"I don't know," she replied, "she never told me."

"Did she ever tell you about someone named Ron?"

"No, she never mentioned that name."

"Thank you, Miss Adams, you've been a big help."

When I reached the lobby of the hospital, I found a pay phone and called Mr. Watson. "Mr. Watson, Jack Stevens. I have a couple more questions."

"Okay."

"Did you wife say anything to you about a lump in her breast?"

"No, who said she did?"

"Miss Adams, at the hospital said Emily told her a few weeks before she disappeared."

"Emily was real fond of Miss Adams." he replied. "When Emily's Mother died, Miss Adams became like a mother to Emily."

"What did Emily's Mother die from?"

He replied with one word, "Cancer."

"One more question. Where is Dr. Jenkins' office?"

"On Main Street in Russell, Kentucky."

I left the hospital and headed for Dr. Jenkins' office. When I approached the receptionist, I told her who I was and that I wanted to see the Doctor

"He's not in today," she replied.

"May I ask where he is?"

"He went deer hunting. Deer season's in and he's a real big deer hunter. Anytime he kills a deer, he brings in a lot of venison to us and sometimes he gives it to the needy."

"Is there any way I can get in touch with him today?"

"I'm sorry Mr. Stevens; I don't even know where he went hunting."

"Maybe you can help me. I need some information on Emily Watson. She came to the Doctor, the day she disappeared. Do you know why she came to see him?"

"I'm not supposed to say this, but you look like an honest man. I remember the day she came in. She and I talked for a while because she was a few minutes early for her appointment. Emily was the last patient for the day. We talked about family and stuff. She told me the boys were growing like weeds. You know, Doctor Jenkins delivered those two babies. Anyway, Emily said she had a cold and wanted some medicine to make her feel better."

"Did Mrs. Watson say anything about having a lump in her breast?"

"Heavens no," she replied.

"I have a big favor to ask of you, Miss Bennett, is it? Can I take a peek at Mrs. Watson's records?"

"Oh gosh, I don't think so. Dr. Jenkins would have my head on a platter if he found out."

"I won't tell him and it would be a big help in trying to locate Mrs. Watson."

Miss Bennett asked, "Do you think she is still alive?"

"I don't know, that's what I'm trying to find out."

"You know, that stuff is confidential. I've probably said too much already. You won't tell Dr. Jenkins what I've told you, will you?"

"No Ma'am. I am bound by confidentiality. When someone tells me something in confidence, I keep it a secret. Like I said, I'm just trying to find out what happened to Mrs. Watson. Her husband and boys need to know, one way or the other and I'm trying to help them."

"If I let you see the file, you won't tell on me, will you?"

"Absolutely not, I'm not trying to get anyone in trouble. We can do enough of that on our own. I certainly don't need help in that area. My lips are sealed."

Miss Bennett turned around and took a file out of a cabinet marked, Dead Files. I thought it was ironic, because I felt Mrs. Watson was already dead. The file revealed nothing that I thought would help me in my search. The records showed a few scrapes and bruises in Emily's younger years. A broken arm was recorded when she was in her late teens. The report said she fell off a bicycle. A few colds and a bout with anemia rounded out the file.

"Thank you Miss Bennett. This is our secret, okay?"

"I'm not going to tell anyone," she replied.

"Me neither," I said, "You've been a big help. Oh by the way, does the Doctor make any calls at the hospital in Ashland?"

"Sometimes," she replied.

Chapter 10

Since it was late in the afternoon and I'd missed lunch, I went across the street to a little diner. Sitting there enjoying my meal, I noticed a car pull up in front of the Doctor's office. I thought good, the Doctor must be back from his hunting trip. I was surprised when I saw Mr. Watson get out of the car. About that time, Miss Bennet, stepped out of the Doctor's office, stopped and locked the door. They met in the middle of the sidewalk and kissed. I mumbled, under my breath, "That's a development neither of them told me about." Those two would merit a closer look. It is possible the husband could have killed Emily, but what would be the connection to the other murders?

After spending the night at a local motel, I drove over to Summit, Kentucky. Jim Stone, the oldest of the missing persons, disappeared about three months after Emily Watson. Stone was a bachelor and as far as I could tell, he did not have any family around. A neighbor said he thought Stone was from New Hampshire and according to the neighbor; Mr. Stone had a disability from a back injury that kept him from working a full time job. Would he go to the hospital for physical therapy? If so, that would tie two of the victims to the hospital. I checked with another neighbor, William Cummins, and he said he took Stone a couple of time to the hospital for therapy. He didn't know why the therapy was necessary because he sat outside and waited. Stone survived on a small pension and that along with the occasional odd job was all he needed to survive. No family ever filed a missing persons report, just the neighbor. The local police went through his apartment and found little information of use. Looks like Mr. Stone was secretive about his past and almost as secretive about his time in Summit. Had the neighbor not filed a missing persons report, Mr. Stone would have very little to prove his existence. Was he trying to hide his past and was he keeping his present life a secret. It would be very interesting to find out just what kind of a disability he had. A call to the New Hampshire State Police was in order. After twenty minutes of getting the run around, I was connected with the Superintendent of the New Hampshire State Police. He told me that Jim Stone was a small time hood and left the state when things started getting a little to hot for him. There were several charges against him. Most of them were minor but there was a possibility of Jim getting into something more serious. Jim was the low man on the totem pole in a criminal organization. The police had turned him and for his information he was given the chance to get out of town or stick around and be taken down with the organization. The bad back was just a cover story given to Stone. Jim took the smart choice and left the state and headed south. How he ended up in Kentucky will always be a mystery as Jim didn't have any friends in the Blue Grass State.

The third missing person was a female named Jane Ulster of Cannonsburg, Kentucky. I was able to contact Jane Ulster's mother, Evelyn Waugh. Mrs. Waugh told me about Jane's divorce. Because Jane was unable to have children, her self worth was very low and when her husband, Richard, left her for that reason, she kind of went off the deep end. Jane worked for a local real estate office after the divorce. She missed so much time; the Realtor had to let her go. After that, Mrs. Waugh said Jane quit taking care of herself. No make up, hair unkempt, and a drastic weight loss, with all the other stress, took its toll on Jane. Jane was reported missing about nine months after Jim Stone. Her Mother felt sure she had taken off, settled down somewhere and started a new life.

Mrs. Waugh, may I ask you a few questions?"

"Yes," she replied.

"Did Jane ever try to find out why she couldn't have children?"

Again she replied, "Yes."

"Do you mind telling me what she found out?"

"No, I don't mind. The Doctor said her womb wasn't developed enough to bear children."

"Do you know the Doctor's name?"

"No, I don't but she went to the Ashland Hospital to see him."

"Did Jane ever try to contact you after she vanished?"

"No."

"I don't mean to be insensitive, but what made you think she ran away?"

"I'll tell you something, Mr. Stevens. A mother has to keep hope that her child is still alive. She was such a sweet girl before all this ugliness happened."

"I'm sure she was Ma'am."

"Mr. Stevens, if you met her before all this happened, you would have liked her. She was such a sweet girl. She was so bubbly and energetic. It seemed to spill out on everyone she was around."

"After the divorce, did she make new friends or go out much?"

"No, she just stayed home or went to work. After she got fired, she stayed home most of the time, and went downhill from there. She went to Wink's Bar and Grill sometimes."

"How was her health?"

"Do you mean was she sick or anything like that?"

"Yes Ma'am." I replied.

"She was radiant before all this happened. Was she sick? Not physically, mentally maybe."

"Do you know if she went to a Doctor for depression?"

"Not that I know of."

I gave her my card and asked her to call me if she remembered anything else that might help.

Number 4 was Raymond Strong. He was a fireman in Catlettsburg, Kentucky. At 42, he was pushing the upper age limit of the missing. Mr. Strong had been a fireman for twenty one years and was required to take an annual physical. He was in the process of retiring for years served. According to his Chief, he had passed a physical to drive a school bus part time. The Fire Chief said he did not know of anyone that did not like Mr. Strong and the last Doctor's report showed he was in excellent health.

"May I ask what Doctor?"

"Sure, he saw Dr. Mendez at the Ashland Hospital."

From what I could gather, Mr. Strong had no known enemies. Someone didn't like him or he would not have disappeared with out a trace.

Number 5 was a farmer from Sybene, Ohio, Tom Castle. He was 41 years old when he was reported missing by his Mother. After Tom's Dad passed away, at the age of 87, Tom and his Mother continued to run the farm. After Tom's disappearance, his Mother quit farming and rented the land out to sharecroppers. What land she didn't sharecrop, was sold off to supplement her meager Social Security. She was in her late seventies and wasn't in the best of health. Her husband's death took a lot of spunk out of her. When Tom disappeared, that was the straw that broke the camel's back. I tried to connect Tom to the Ashland Hospital but his Mother said he went a Doctor in

Chesapeake, Ohio and that Doctor frequented the Huntington Hospital. I think the bad memories were just too much for her to bear and she just discontinued the farming operation. I thanked Mrs. Castle her for her time and moved on.

Number 6 was Ed Hopkins, age 39. He was from Chesapeake, Ohio and operated a local hardware store that closed up a few months before his disappearance. He had been missing the shortest amount of time, three months. When I talked to his wife, she told me he was a proud man and he really took it hard when he went bankrupt. When he closed the store, fourteen people lost their jobs. "Mrs. Hopkins, was he depressed enough to leave?"

"He did not leave," she said vehemently, "He was a proud man and vowed someday he would be back on top. I know my husband. Something has happened to him. I just wish I knew."

"Mrs. Hopkins, did he make any of his employees mad when he had to close the store?'

"No, he had a meeting the last day and apologized to everyone, I was there, too. Just about everyone was in tears when he locked the door for the last time. No, no one was mad, we were all sad. The employees had been with Tom for many years and they all loved him. He was a good boss. He treated everyone just like brothers and sisters."

"Did any of them owe Tom any money?"

"Yes, a few did, but it wasn't more than a couple of

hundred dollars all together. Tom would let them buy what they needed and take it out of their paychecks a little at a time."

"How long after the bankruptcy did Tom disappear?"

"About two weeks after it was final."

"How did he feel about the bankruptcy?"

"Not good, but he got a job at the farm bureau store and was selling a lot because he knew everyone. In fact, sometimes, he would bring home more money than he made at the hardware store. Tom would make sure everybody else got paid at the hardware store before he would pay himself. If it was a slow week at the hardware store, Tom wouldn't take a pay check."

"When did he disappear?"

"Three months ago, last week. He got home from work around 7:30 PM and said he was going to take a walk before supper. He never returned home. I miss him Mr. Stevens."

"I'm sure you do, Mrs. Hopkins. I'm going to do my best to find him." I left my card and told her the same as I told the others, "Call if you think of anything that might help."

The only thing the six had in common was that they were all missing. Four of the six had connections to the Ashland Hospital. The other two would probably go to the hospital in Huntington, West Virginia.

My next step was to check on Ron something or other working at the hospital in Ashland. I called the employment department and was referred to Mr. T.J

McElroy, Director of Employment. I called and made an appointment to see him at 10:00 AM Tuesday morning. After introducing myself, I told him I was investigating some missing person's reports and several of the missing had been in his hospital over a period of time.

"In fact," I told him, "One of them actually worked here. Does the name Emily Watson ring a bell?"

"Yes." he replied, "Emily worked here for a number of years."

"I have one other name that I'd like to run by you. Does the name Ron mean anything to you?"

"Yes it does. We had a technician by that name and maybe a couple of orderlies."

"I'd be interested in the full names of those employees."

"Okay Mr. Stevens, I'll have to do some checking and let you know."

"Thanks," I said, I'll be back in a couple of days."

Friday, I revisited Mr. McElroy and he had two names for me, Ron Issacs and Ron Templeton. According to Mr. McElroy, Issacs quit several months ago but Templeton was still employed and was scheduled to for duty at 3:00 PM. Since it was 1:30, I decided to grab a bite to eat and return at 3:00 o'clock to talk to Templeton. Mr. McElroy called Templeton in the office and I began questioning him around 3:15. "Ron, I'm investigating the disappearance of Emily Watson. Did you know her?"

"Yeah, I saw her around the hospital a few times."

"Did you ever talk to her?"

"No, she was married."

"Did you find her attractive?"

"Yeah, but I told you she was married, besides that I don't fool around with women."

"What do you mean, Ron?"

"You know, I'm...you know."

Then it hit me, he was homosexual. Being homosexual did not eliminate him as a suspect in Emily's disappearance.

I left the hospital and headed back to the office. I had to have Dickerson run the two guys through the system to see if they had any kind of a record. Isaacs had been around the area for years and Templeton, originally from California, came east about a year before Emily disappeared. Templeton had a few charges on his record of public indecency, involving homosexual acts in public and a couple of reckless driving charges for speeding. Isaacs on the other hand was a horse of another color. His rap sheet was as long as my arm. Most were petty theft and other minor charges. Three assault and battery charges were of major importance. Both men were possible suspects but Isaacs was the most probable.

I had to find Isaacs and my first step was to get back to McElroy to attempt to get an address. "Mr. McElroy, do you know where Isaacs went after he left here?"

"I don't know for sure but I heard he ended up in a hospital in Charleston, West Virginia. Why do you want to know?"

"Did you know he had a police record?"

"No, I didn't," he replied.

"Don't you check the background on your employees before you hire them?"

"Yes, we normally do, but he came highly recommended."

"By whom,' I asked?

"By Ron Templeton."

"I need Templeton's address," I said.

"I'm sorry, but it's against hospital policy to give out employee addresses."

I was able to get Templeton's address by threatening to bring in a court order and then leaking the information to a newspaper.

I returned to the office and told Dickerson I was going to Huntington to do a stake out on Templeton's apartment. Two days later, I saw Templeton pull up around 7:00 PM and about a half hour later, another car pulled in the parking spot next to Templetons's car. I called the local police for back up and about fifteen minutes later; we busted in and caught them in a compromising position. "Templeton, who's your partner?"

"I'm Ron Isaacs, why do you want to know? You interested in a little action?"

"I'll show you some action. I'll dance all over your head with these size 11's. Get your damn clothes on, you're going to jail for questioning. And while we're at it Templeton, you get dressed too. You're also going in for questioning."

Back at the Huntington Police Department, I interviewed Isaacs. "I think you know something about the disappearance of Emily Watson and maybe a few more missing persons"

He replied, "I don't know what the hell you're talking about."

"You and Templeton worked at the same hospital as Emily. Templeton's record is relatively minor stuff, but yours is another story. I feel Emily met with foul play and I think you and Templeton had something to do with it. A few weeks before she disappeared she told her husband she had some trouble with someone named Ron who worked at the hospital."

"Yeah, I did have some trouble with her, but I didn't do anything to her."

"What kind of trouble did you have?"

"I hit on her and she got real snotty with me and called me a queer."

"Well, aren't you?"

"Hell no," he replied, "I swing both ways."

"What did you do after she called you that name?"

"I started messing with her, calling her names and changing orders on her patients. I wanted it to look like she messed up. I would have done anything to make her look bad."

"Including murder?"

"Hell no, I didn't do anything like that."

"Where were you on February 28, 1962?"

"Hell," he said, "That was along time ago. The 28th is my Mother's birthday and I visited her because it was her birthday. I even took a day off work to drive to Morehead, where she lives. Templeton went with me and we spent the night at Mom's house. That was the first time I saw her since I came back from California. Why is that date so important to you?"

"That's the day Emily Watson disappeared. I'm going to hold you and Templeton until I check out your alibi and if your alibi is solid, you will be free to go do what ever you guys do."

The next morning, I drove to Morehead and found Mrs. Walter Issacs in the phone book. After getting directions, I drove out to her house, which was about two miles out of town on Peterson Road. It was a little white cottage that needed some touching up. A white picket fence surrounded the house and hid the yard that was bit overgrown. I went up the sidewalk and knocked on the door. When the door opened, a little old white haired lady asked me what I wanted. "Are you Mrs. Walter Issacs?"

"Yes, who's asking?"

"Ma'am, my name is Jack Stevens. I'm a federal investigator and I need to know when your son, Ron, came to visit after he returned from California"

"Why, is he in trouble?"

"I don't know yet, but it is very important, for your son's sake, I find out when you saw him after he returned from California."

"February 28, 1962. That was my birthday and that is the only time he ever comes to see me; once a year on my birthday. That was the first time he brought his queer friend with him. When they decided to spend the night, I made them sleep in different rooms. I told Ronald he is welcome to come anytime but to never bring his friend again."

"Ma'am, was his friend Ron Templeton?"

"Yes, that's his name."

I drove back to Huntington and told the chief, "Turn them loose, their alibi checks out."

Damn, I was back to square one. I had to start all over and the first step was to double check to be sure no one had shown up anywhere else in the country. Going back to Dickerson, I had him run the names, again, through the FBI network. Another check on the social security numbers revealed that all payments had ceased when the persons were reported missing. Finger prints were not readily available for the missing and all that would show was that the missing persons had not been in any trouble prior to being reported missing.

The six people did not have much of anything in common. In fact, all I could see in common was that they were all missing. I had to double check to make sure none of the above had shown up anywhere else in the country. A week later, Dickerson ran the names through the FBI network again. Social security numbers were double checked to make sure no one was paying SS taxes on the numbers. About two weeks later, we re-confirmed that the payment of SS taxes ceased when the persons were reported missing. After we finally got finger prints on a couple of the missing, Jim Stone and Raymond Strong, they did not match up with anything the FBI had on file. This only showed the people missing had not been in any prior trouble with the law, except for Jim Strong After a month of wheel spinning, I told Dickerson I had to do something. I was puzzled as to what, but I had to try something.

Chapter 11

I retraced my steps to the missing person's towns in the circle. The Victorian house had begun to reappear in my dreams. Every town, I drove through, I'd stop and seek out a real estate agent. Somebody had to have knowledge of that house and I certainly would not find it if I sat on my ass. Late fall; in the little town of Flatwoods, Kentucky, I hit pay dirt. Bryan Hartwicke, of Hartwicke Realty, informed me of a place similar to the one I described to him. Bryan gave me directions to the house and told me, "Since it's getting late in the day, you may want to wait until morning to find it. You'll be able to see it better in daylight and it's a forty five minute drive."

"I have to see it tonight," I replied. As I pulled out of Flatwoods, I was filled with fear and trepidation. I wanted to find that house but did I really want to confront what ever evil was inside waiting for me.

After sixty minutes of driving, I was hopelessly lost. Bryan told me it was a long gravel drive through some trees. It sounded exactly like my dream. I turned around and headed back, berating myself for getting lost and not waiting for morning. After ten minutes, I spotted a gravel drive off to my right. I was unable to see it when I passed earlier because the trees were almost blocking the drive when I came from the other direction. I parked on the edge of the road and walked over to the stand of trees. The full moon barely illuminated the gate across the driveway. A chain was padlocked around the gate and a post. The chain was old and rusty but the padlock seemed have to less rust on it. "Hell, walking's not crowded," I uttered out loud as I climbed over the gate. The driveway disappeared into the woods and as I started walking back the driveway, something ran across the driveway about three feet in front of me. It scared the hell out of me and my heart was pounding in my chest. It was beating so hard, I thought I could hear it. What ever it was went crashing through the woods as an owl in the distance gave an ominous, whoooo, whoooo. Every step I took was met with spider webs stretched across in front of me. When I wasn't wiping spider webs from my face, the bushes overgrowing the driveway were tearing at my clothes and skin. It felt like a thousand hands were grabbing at me, trying to keep me away from the house. Maybe it was a warning to stay out. Several months ago, a vision from Barbara, warned me, "Be careful, it is full of evil."

An icy chill ran up my spine and I visibly shuddered. Again, I spoke out loud, "Jack, you're stupid, come back during the day light." Something compelled me forward like I was being drawn to the evil. The evening was chilly but I could feel the sweat dripping down my back. After several minutes, I stepped out of the woods into a large clearing. There in the middle of the clearing, illuminated by moonlight, sat my nightmare. Do I proceed or do I run? Whatever evil was inside that house beckoned me, like a moth to the flame. With leaden feet, I proceeded towards the house. My breathing was labored and the fear of the unknown ran rampant through my mind. When I touched the front gate latch, a mist appeared on the overgrown lawn and rose up to form six ghostly hollowed eyed and open mouthed apparitions. The screams of dying people and the gasping for breath assailed my mind. When I opened the gate, the apparitions dissipated in the mist and each step I took towards the house echoed in the stillness.

When I reached the front porch steps, I stopped. Moonlight bathed the front of the house and when I looked up, I saw a gargoyle on each corner of the house. Each one was the face of evil with fangs protruding from their mouths and wings sprouting from their backs. Long talons protruded from each paw and curled over the edge of the roof. I felt they could come to life at any minute and spring at me. My throat would be torn open and I'd probably be disemboweled. Shaking that feeling, I stepped up on the porch. The floor boards squeaked as I trod on them. Turning the door knob failed to gain me entry to the house and true to my dreams; I turned to my right and noticed a piece of plywood covering a window. It was bowed out on one side, like it was taunting me. It was my nightmare coming true. I walked over and started pulling on it and soon I was able to remove enough to check the window. It was unlocked and I raised the window and slipped inside. In the pitch black, I struck a match and all I could see were long white fangs. In my haste to jump out of the way, I dropped the match. When it did not attack me in a few seconds, I got up the nerve to light another match. The damned thing was a stuffed bear almost seven feet tall. When that match burned out, I lit another and looked around. On my left, was a candle in a wall sconce that I promptly lit. It gave a little more light than the match. All the furniture in the room was draped with white cloth. Finding another candle and lighting it, illuminated several stuffed animal heads on the walls and just like the bear, they were all showing fangs.

I'd seen enough snarling fangs and opened the door into the hallway. There appeared to be a sitting room across the hall from the animal room. As I continued down the hall, I noticed a closed door on my left. I twisted the knob and entered the room. After looking around for a few minutes, I was getting ready to continue with my exploration of my nightmare when a glint of something caught my eye. I walked over and discovered a chest with the following items on it:

1—Pocket knife

1—Fountain pen

2—Unmatched earrings

1—Ladies necklace

1—Food stamp
1—Wrist watch
1—Key

Instinctively, I snatched up the items, wrapped them in my handkerchief and jammed them in my pocket. The chest was dust free, unlike the other rooms I'd been in. Then I noticed a candle at each end of the chest. It looked like it was an altar for the items. As I started out of the room, I heard a slight noise to my left and started to turn when someone or something grabbed me by the throat. I dropped the candles and started fighting for my life. That thing had such grip on my throat that I couldn't break free. I was beginning to lose consciousness and in a desperate last struggle, I brought my knee up to its groin. If this thing was male, it had to have balls. My knee connected and I heard it scream as it released me from its deadly grip. I kneed it again and another scream came from its throat. As it dropped to the floor, I was struggling to get my breath. Shaking off the effects of the strangling, I started for it. It scooted backwards and all of a sudden, it jumped up and ran for the window. The window shattered in a shower of wood and glass. I quickly looked around the room and saw the only door was blocked by growing flames. My only exit was the same window it jumped out so I ran over to the window and looked out. I certainly hoped it was not out there waiting for me to come out the window. When I looked out the window, I saw it disappearing into the woods on the north side of the house. Jumping out the window, I took off running for my car to the south. There was no way I was following that damn thing into the woods at night. Once I reached my car, my breathing returned to normal. From the safety of my car, I could see the sky take on an orange glow. The whole house would probably be in flame soon. I fired up my car and headed back to Russell, Kentucky.

I spent the night in a local motel. My sleep was interrupted with nightmares of that thing chasing me. As soon as the court house was opened the next morning, I went in and walked down the hall to the property tax division. After talking to an official and showing my badge, I was given the cooperation I needed. A clerk told me, "The house is still shown in the estate of Evangeline Jenkins, but she died about twenty years ago."

"Have the property taxes been paid since she died?"

"Yes sir," she replied.

"By whom." I asked.

"Robert Jenkins pays every year, just like clock work. Evangeline was his Mother."

"Thank you Ma'am."

Leaving the courthouse, I headed straight to Dr. Robert Jenkins' office. When I walked in, the receptionist gave me a look of fear. I knew she was concerned about me telling the Doctor of our little conversation a while back. When I approached the desk, I told her, "Don't worry; the other day is still our secret. Could you tell the Doctor a Federal

Agent is here to see him?"

"Yes sir, right away."

She left and returned in a couple of minutes and said the Doctor would be right out.

"I'm Robert Jenkins, how may I help you?"

"Thanks for taking the time to see me," I replied. "I'm investigating the disappearance of Emily Watson. It appears to have been a kidnapping and we investigate all kidnappings."

"I'll be glad to help in any way I can," he said.

"Emily was your patient for a number of years, right?"

"Yes, she had been coming to me since she was a teenager."

"Did she have any distinguishing marks of scars?"

"Just the scar on her right elbow. I had to put a pin in it when she broke her arm, other than that, no."

"Did she have any birth marks or any thing else that might identify her?"

"No. She was very healthy except for a bout with anemia a few years ago."

I thanked him and stuck out my hand to shake his. I was amazed at the size of his hands, much bigger than mine. As he walked away, he seemed to be walking gingerly.

"You're limping Doctor, did you hurt yourself?"

"Yeah, I was hunting the other day and fell."

"Thanks for you time, Doctor."

There was something evil about the good Doctor. I

didn't know what it was but there was something about him that oozed evil.

I left the Doctor's office and decided I better let Dickerson know where I am and what is going on. "Dickerson, it's me, Jack."

"Where in the hell are you, Jack?"

"In Russell, Kentucky, I think I've found our strangler."

I filled Dickerson in on everything that I did over the last couple of weeks. When I told him I needed a court order to dig on Evangeline Jenkins' farm, he asked,

"Why Jack?"

"I know you won't believe me but there are at least six bodies buried there"

"And just how in the hell do you know that?"

"Dickerson, you wouldn't believe me if I told you. You just have to trust me on this one."

"Okay Jack, you haven't been wrong on your hunches yet. I'll get a Federal Judge to issue an exhumation order. I'll see you tomorrow. Where are you staying?"

"At a motel called Johnson's on Main Street."

After I finished talking to Dickerson, I went to a little greasy spoon to get something to eat. All I could do was wait on Dickerson, but something gave me an uneasy feeling about spending another night in the motel. After eating, I jumped on the beast and drove about twenty miles before pulling into another motel. I wanted to put some distance between me and the Doctor.

I was back in Russell around 8:30 AM and spent the

next three hours waiting for Dickerson to show up. When he pulled in around noon, we went straight to the police department. They in turn contacted the County Coroner. By 3:00 PM. we had a back hoe lined up and everyone was on the way to the Jenkins' farm. When we got there, the house had burned to the ground. Little pockets of glowing embers sent tendrils of smoke skyward. "Come on Dickerson, walk with me." As I walked the property, there were areas where I would feel a sense of dread come over me. I would stop and ask Dickerson to lay a piece of charred wood on the ground by me feet.

"Jack, what the hell are you doing?"

"I don't know, Dickerson, just lay the damn wood down like I ask you to do. Tell the back hoe operator to start digging here. He should find something a few feet down."

By 5:00 o'clock, we had discovered three sets of bones. The Police chief sent one of his deputies back to get some emergency lighting. With the lights illuminating the yard, we discovered a total of three more bodies buried on the property. The Coroner bagged and tagged each set of bones as human. Now, the task of identifying the remains was our next priority. Dickerson volunteered to stay and oversee that project. I told him I appreciated that, as I had things to do. My job was to get the mementos of the killers to each family involved and see if they could recognize any of the items. While Dr. Jenkins was our prime suspect, we did not have any proof he was the killer.

I left for Ashland. Mr. Watson was coming out of his

house when I pulled up. The boys and Ms. Bennett were with him. “Mr. Watson, I have some things I want you to look at and tell me if you recognize any of them. When I unrolled the package, his mouth dropped open.

“That earring was Emily’s. I gave it to her four years ago. By the way, this is not what you think it is. We’re just good friends.”

“Mr. Watson, you don’t have to explain anything to me. Miss Bennett is a very nice lady and I’m sure your wife would approve. You still have two young boys to raise and they need a mother. Now I have to tell you the hard part. I found these items in a house outside Russell. We found six sets of bones buried in the yard. I need to know your wife’s dentist so we can get dental records and try to match them to the bodies we found.”

He was crying and between sobs, he managed to say, “Dr. Martin.”

“Miss Bennett, he and the boys need you.”

As she hugged him, I walked off. One down and five to go.

After driving for a half hour, I was sitting in front of the house of Jim Stone‘s neighbor. He identified the fountain pen as belonging to Jim Stone. Two down and four to go.

Mrs. Waugh identified the other earring as belonging to Jane Ulster. Three down and three to go.

The Fire Chief in Catlettsburg identified the pocket knife as one he had seen Raymond Strong use many times. Four down and two to go.

Tom Castle's wife identified the pocket watch. She said Tom carried it for years and that his father carried it for many years before he gave it to Tom. Five down and one to go.

Mrs. Hopkins identified the key as the key to the hardware store her husband had to close. She said it was the only memento he kept of the store. That made number six.

I had one item left, the necklace. We may never know who he killed to get the necklace or the food stamp.

I was back in Russell the next day carrying dental records for every one except Jim Stone. The coroner matched dental records for five of the victims. The remains of Jim Stone were identified through the process of elimination. The Coroner said the bone structure, of the last body, was consistent with the age and size of Jim Stone. I told Dickerson of my suspicions about Doctor Jenkins and gave him the items I found in the house. "Take them back and check them for finger prints. My plan is to watch him for a while. All we have now is circumstantial and we need more to nail him. He needs to kill and he will eventually make a mistake. When he does, I'll be there to nail his ass to the barn door."

CHAPTER 12

Doctor Jenkins was unmarried and had his living quarters over his office. Since he was a respectful member of society, I didn't think he would act up during the day. If he was committing these murders, he would need the cover of darkness to do his evil deeds. I kept my room at the motel and reversed my sleeping habits. Staying awake at night was a little rough getting used to, but it was a price I was willing to pay. After two weeks, Dr. Evans was still behaving himself. Maybe I was wrong. Maybe it was someone else doing the killing. Near the end of the second week, I was leaving my room when Mr. Watson and Miss Bennett were coming out of the motel office. They were hand in hand as they walked towards me. They were so engrossed with each other; they did not see me until they almost bumped into me. When they recognized me, they looked like a couple of kids who had been caught with their hands in the cookie jar. Miss Bennett tried to speak, "Mr. Stevens, I...we...I mean...this is not what it seems,"

Watson spoke up, "Yeah, it's not like that."

"Listen," I said, "You two evidently care for each other." Looking at Watson, I continued, "It's been more than two years since your wife's been gone. That's a respectable mourning period. You two need to quit hiding your feelings for each other. Miss Bennett, you can never replace the boy's Mother, but you can be the best dammed Step Mom in the world."

They didn't know what to say. We all stood there for a couple of awkward moments until Watson spoke up, "Jack, what are you still doing in town?'

"I need you two to keep quiet about seeing me. There's still something about this case I haven't nailed down."

Miss Bennett asked, "What, who killed all those people?"

"Yes," I replied. "You have to keep my presence a secret. There are future lives depending on you to keep it a secret. The killer of those six people has to feel that the Feds have left town. He has to think he has free reign to continue his evil ways."

"Okay," they replied in unison, "We'll keep your secret if you'll keep ours."

"You got a deal," I replied, as I left to spend the night in an alley, again, watching Dr. Jenkins.

It seemed night after night; Dr. Jenkins would close his office at 5:00 PM, go upstairs to his living quarters and spend the rest of the night there. Things changed in late September. After spending a few hours in his living quarters, he would slip out. As I followed him each time it seemed like he scouting for a victim. This continued for almost a week, until Friday night when he came out of the apartment dressed in dark slacks and a dark shirt. I thought, you evil bastard, you're up to no good.

I followed him very closely, my headlights off. The moon was full and I could see well enough to drive without the headlights. I could stay close to him and he wouldn't even know I was back there. He headed south east out of town and stayed on the back roads until he got to the skid row section of Ashland, Kentucky. Jenkins parked his car and started walking towards the flood wall. I parked about a half block behind him and followed, staying in the shadows so he could not see me. After working my way to within a hundred feet of him, he stopped and slipped into the shadows himself. About a hundred feet past him, I noticed someone staggering down the sidewalk. When that person got to where Jenkins was waiting, Jenkins emerged from the shadows and snatched the victim back into the shadows with him.

I could see Jenkins move towards an alley, dragging the victim with him. I took off at a fast run and hit Evans with a flying tackle. We rolled around on the ground until he hit me twice and stunned me. While I was out of it for a couple of seconds, he jumped up and ran in a vacant building. Shaking off the effects of the punches, I scrambled to my feet and started in after him. Inside the building, I heard heavy breathing. The moon light shining in the windows illuminated what had been some sort of a machine shop. Several pieces of machinery looked like old band saws and gave the appearance of giant insects in the moonlight. An idle conveyor ran over head with big hooks dangling from it. A heavy metal door was barely visible on the other side of the room. Drawing on an inner reserve of strength, I started through the door.

About ten feet inside the room, I felt a tremendous blow on the back. I fell in a heap and fought the urge to pass out. Next thing I knew, Jenkins was on top of me with his hands around my throat. He mumbled, “If I can’t have the other person, you will do nicely.”

As his fingers tightened around my throat, I prayed, Barbara, I need your help.

A bright light filled the room. Jenkins was caught off guard and I was able to get my foot in his gut. I kicked with every ounce of strength I could muster. Jenkins flew through the air, hitting the wall with a loud thud. He sat there a few seconds, as if the wind had been knocked out of him. When he regained his composure, he reached for the door jamb to help himself get up. I knew if he got to me again, he would kill me. He was about half way up when I kicked the heavy metal door closed. It closed with a loud clang and Jenkins screamed. I saw the blood spurting from his right hand. As he bent to strangle me, I kicked him again and this time his head hit the metal door. He fell and lay, unmoving, on the floor. I rolled over, got up and found an old electrical cord. I bound his hands and feet and only after binding him securely, did apply a tourniquet to his right arm.

When he came to, he started screaming, "Let me up, I'll kill you."

"Jenkins, your killing days are over. The only death you will be near again is when they strap you into the electric chair."

The tourniquet stemmed the flow of blood and I left him laying there while I went out to call the local police and Dickerson.

"Dickerson, I got him."

"Jack, where are you?"

"On Front Street in Ashland. The locals will arrive before you. Just look for the flashing lights."

"Okay, stay there, I'll be there in a little while."

The local police pulled up in about five minutes. After talking to me for a few minutes, they went inside to get Jenkins. He was still struggling and screaming when they stood him upright. One of the locals asked,

"Stevens, what happened to his right hand?"

"Got slammed in a door. Looks like he got a nasty gash on it. You might want to run him by the hospital and have it looked at."

"Gash hell," he replied, "all four fingers have been severed."

"In that case, you'll probably find the fingers on the other side of that metal door," I replied.

By that time, Dickerson rolled up. After explaining everything to him, he gave me an update on the six victims. All six had been positively identified and reburied. The trinkets from the house of Evangeline Jenkins were checked for finger prints. The pocket watch, the pocket knife and the fountain pen had partial prints but they were good enough for a match to Jenkins. "Good job Jack, take a couple days off and come in on Monday. We'll find something else for you to do."

Jenkins was sitting in the cruiser by this time and I had a couple of questions I wanted to ask him. "Dickerson, there's a couple of questions I have to ask him. Come with me so I won't be tempted to kill him."

"Okay Jack, lead the way."

I walked over and opened the rear door of the cruiser. Jenkins had quieted down and seemed to a little more lucid. "Jenkins, why did you put nickels on the eyes of the victims?"

He looked at me and replied, "So they could have a little traveling money."

"What in the hell do you mean, traveling money?"

You mean Jack Stevens don't know everything?"

"No Jenkins, I don't know everything, enlighten me."

"Legend is, in Greek Mythology, the family put coins on the eyes of the dead to pay the God Charon, for the ferry ride to the under world. So they had to have traveling money."

"That doesn't explain why you killed all those people."

"I don't know why," he replied. "I guess I just enjoyed ridding the world of the unworthy,"

"Did you kill the three in Ironton?"

"Yes." he replied.

"Why didn't you bury them like the others? You probably could have gotten away with it for years."

"The newspapers listed the first six as missing, they weren't missing and I wanted the world to know of my work "

"One last question. The necklace, who did it belong to? How about the food stamp?"

Evans hung his head and replied, "My mother and the hobo in Ironton."

"Did you kill them?"

When he replied, "Yes," I saw a tear in the corner of his eye.

After he said that, I dug through my pockets and pulled out a couple of nickels. I stuck them in his shirt pocket and told him. "Here, take these. It's your traveling money. Carry it with you when you walk your last mile, just before they fry you in the electric chair. Oh, there's one thing you didn't realize."

"Yeah," he replied, "What's that?"

"The ferry is coming for you. Those nickels are your traveling money."

CHAPTER 13

Monday morning, I stopped at the Ironton PD before reporting to work. When

I entered the station; it was like I was in a tomb. My old partner, Don Hamilton, was no where to be seen. I asked the desk sergeant, “Where’s Don?”

“Jeez Jack, I’m sorry I’m the one to tell you this but Don was assassinated last night. He pulled the evening shift in the south end of town. When he didn’t report at the end of his shift, we tried to reach him by radio. It was pushing midnight and still no answer. That’s when we sent a couple of cars out looking for him. We searched every street in the south end of town and everywhere else we could think of. Around 2:00 AM, Grady Hicks found him at the old gravel pit, off Third Street.”

I became highly agitated and began asking questions. “Who? Why? What happened? What’s being done? Do you have any suspects?”

I had a thousand more questions but was interrupted by the desk sergeant. “Jack, I don’t know the answer to any of those questions.”

“Where’s Hicks, I want to talk to him.”

"He's up at the crime scene."

"Where's Sanchez?"

"He's in the office with Dickerson."

"Excuse me, I'm going in there."

Sanchez and Dickerson looked grim when I entered the office. Sanchez looked like he hadn't slept all night and had a five o'clock shadow at 8:30 in the morning. Dickerson didn't look any better.

"Okay guys, tell me what's being done to catch Don's killer."

Dickerson spoke up, "Sit down, Jack. Right now, we're just trying to make heads or tails out of this."

"Do we know what happened?"

Sanchez filled me in on what they thought happened. "Don must have been surprised while he was on patrol. When we found him, the passenger door was unlocked and Don's paper work was thrown in the back seat. We suspect the person forced Don, at gun point, to drive to the gravel pit. There were foot prints from the passenger side of the car around to the drivers' side. Don's foot prints from the car joined the other set of foot prints and they walked about twenty feet from the car. You can see where Don was forced to kneel and then he was shot in the back of the head. What really pisses me off was that after shooting him, they ripped out his throat."

"What kind of maniac are we dealing with" I asked?

Dickerson chimed in, "We don't know Jack, but we need to get him and get him quick."

"Are there any clues" I inquired?

Sanchez replied, "We have two things. Number one, it had to be a large caliber weapon. We suspect a large bore hand gun, possibly with a silencer. The bullet entered the back of his head and damn near tore off half his face. The hole in the back of his head was too small for a shot gun. Besides that, someone would have heard the blast from a shot gun, especially with Moore's being that close. Number two is the foot prints on the passenger side of the car. We have a crew up there taking a cast of the prints right now."

"Has anyone interviewed the people at Moore's?"

"I have someone up there right now." replied Sanchez.

"Who," I asked?

"Grady Hicks. He partnered with Don while you were on special assignment."

"Why wasn't he with Don last night?"

"We were short handed last night. Grady took a domestic disturbance on North Third Street and Don said he could patrol the south end by himself."

"Is that all we know? I asked.

"I'm afraid that's it."

"Where's Don's body?"

"Over at the coroner's office." replied Dickerson.

"I'm going over there."

The Coroner, George Young, wasn't surprised to see me. "I thought I might see you," he said. "I'm sorry this happened. Don was your partner at one time, wasn't he?"

"Yeah, my first and only partner. I'm going to nail the bastard that did this. Don was a good cop and he will be missed. The person that did this was an animal and when I nail him, he will be treated like the animal he is. Have you had a chance to examine Don's body?

"I'm in the process, Jack. Let me show you a couple of things."

We walked to the room where Don's body lay, covered with a white sheet. When George removed the sheet covering Don's face, or what was left of it, I had to step away, barely reaching a waste can before I relieved myself of my breakfast. Don's chin was the only thing that looked human. The rest of his face was nothing but raw meat. I told George, "Cover him up, I don't want to see him like that, I prefer to remember him as he was."

We started back to his office and once inside the office he told me, "Don was probably killed with a hollow point bullet, possibly a forty five caliber or larger. His throat was ripped out with something, maybe three blades and probably claw like. I could see where the blades punctured left side of his neck. The blades cut about an inch before they started tearing the flesh. The blades were probably sharp for an inch or so and after the initial cut, the rest of the way across his throat was ripped out with brute force."

"Is there anything else you can tell me?"

"Yes, the killer was left handed and Don's throat appeared to be ripped out several minutes after he died as there wasn't much bleeding from that site. Most of the blood on the ground was from his face. The biggest blood pool was several feet from where he was laying. The killer may have even pulled the body back to rip his throat out. If his heart had been beating at the time, there would have been much more blood under his neck. From the angle of the entry wound and if Don was kneeling, the killer is probably five ten to six two. I know it doesn't help much, but that's all I have. If I come up with anything else, I'll call you."

"Thanks George, I'll stay in touch."

I left the coroner's office and headed back to the station. Sanchez and Dickerson were still there and I told them, "I'm going to Moore's to see if Grady found out anything."

"Okay Jack, keep us informed."

When I walked in, Grady was interviewing one of the waitresses. After he looked up and saw me, he looked kind of disappointed that I was there. He finished with the waitress and came over, "Hi Jack, I guess Sanchez decided to send in the big guns."

"No Grady, I'm not a big gun. This is your investigation and all I'm here for is to offer my assistance, if you want it. If not, I'll go back down the road."

Grady looked kind of sheepish and said, "I didn't mean it that way, Jack. Of course, I'll accept your help."

"Good," I replied, "If you ever feel like I'm stepping on your toes, let me know and I'll back off, okay?"

"Okay Jack, thanks."

Grady filled me in on what he had, absolutely nothing. No one saw or heard anything unusual. I was getting ready to suggest we come back and interview the evening shift when Grady asked me to meet him back here at 3:30. When we returned, I was pleasantly surprised to see Rebecca standing behind the counter. “Hello Jack, long time, no see.”

“I know,” I replied, “How are you?”

“I’m fine, getting ready to take my finals in a few weeks. It won’t be long before I graduate.”

“Are you ready for the finals?”

“Yeah, I’m ready.”

“Rebecca, were you working last night?”

“Yes, I was.”

“Did you see anything unusual during your shift?”

“Is this about the cop that was killed last night?”

Grady told her, “Yes, it was an especially brutal murder.”

Rebecca continued, “He was here last night. He had a cup of coffee and a slice of apple pie. I guess it was about 10:15 when he came in. He sat in a booth and about 10:30, someone came in and sat down with him. A little before 11:00 o’clock, they got up and left together.”

Grady asked her, “Did Don seem a little nervous?”

“Not that I noticed.”

“Can you describe the man that left with Don?”

“He was about twenty five years old and probably weighed two hundred pounds; maybe six feet tall. He wasn't fat, just stocky. Blond hair with a ruddy complexion, oh yeah, he had a crew cut. In fact, if Officer Hicks would get a crew cut and dye it blond, put on about twenty pounds, he would resemble that person."

"If you ever saw him again, could you identify him?"

"Oh yes, most definitely."

"Good," I replied, "We will stop by tomorrow with some mug shots. I don't think he's local, but you never know."

We finished interviewing the other waitresses and they agreed with Rebecca's story. Grady and I started out of the restaurant when Rebecca yelled for us to wait a minute.

"One thing I almost forgot. The other guy had a tattoo of a wolf's head on his left forearm. Jack, can I talk to you for a minute?"

"Sure," I replied, as we stepped off to one side.

"When are you going to come back and see me?"

"How about Saturday night? I'll treat to supper at a nice restaurant."

"Okay," she replied.

"Good, I'll pick you up around 7:30."

Tuesday through Friday, I spent most of my time checking on killers that used the same MO as Don's killer. We were able to come up with five names that used the execution style slayings. The suspects were, Anthony Moskowics, Joseph Winters, Adam Tillotson, Willie Sanderson, and MarvinWren. Moskowics and Sanderson were killed three years ago by the same MO as they were used to dishing out. Joseph Winters was still serving time in the Ohio Penitentiary. That left Tillotson and Wren. Tillotson would be in his middle seventies by now so that left Wren as a possible suspect. He had not been seen for three years. Wren was a suspect in a killing in West Virginia over three years ago. The Huntington Police Department brought him in and talked to him but did not have enough evidence to arrest him at the time. When they cut him loose, he just disappeared from the face of the earth. About three months after he disappeared, the police got a break in the case. A sanitation worker found a pistol in sewer on the outskirts of Huntington. The ballistics test showed it to be the weapon that killed a prominent Doctor and the finger prints matched Marvin Wren.

I requested Wren's rap sheet and was surprised as hell when I recognized the picture. I couldn't remember where I saw him but I know that face had popped up somewhere in my life before. I racked my brain until it hurt trying to remember where I saw him.

I reported in for work on Thursday and told Dickerson of my suspicions. "Dickerson, I'm going down to talk to Sanchez. Maybe he's seen this character before."

After I entered the station, I asked the desk sergeant, "Where's Sanchez?"

"He's not here yet, Jack. Should be in shortly."

"Good, I'll wait."

Sanchez showed up about fifteen minutes later and I caught him about five steps inside the door. "Juan, look at this picture and tell me if you have ever seen him before."

After looking at it for a few minutes, Juan said, "Doesn't ring a bell with me."

I told him, "I've seen this bastard before, I just don't remember where."

"Jack, quit thinking about it so hard. You're going to injure your brain. It will come to you eventually."

"I know," I replied, "I just want it sooner than later." Lying in bed that night, it hit me. Just like a bolt out of the blue. When I was partnered with Don, we stopped him on a traffic charge. His name was Winton Craig.

Friday morning, I headed for the Ironton Police Department to tell Sanchez about Mr. Wren, alias Winton Craig. Sanchez had an officer go to the old records and find the ticket Don and I gave Craig. We needed that address. About two hours later, the officer returned with a copy of the ticket. A half hour later, Sanchez, two local officers and I were on our way to pick up Mr. Craig. Craig lived in a trailer home and when we pulled up, I noticed a wheel chair ramp leading up to the front door. The two locals took the back of the home and Sanchez and I took the front. The door would not stop a bullet so Sanchez and I stood off to one side when I knocked on the door. I was surprised when I heard. "Come in." I slowly opened the door and was shocked to see Craig sitting in a wheel chair. In his lap was a pistol.

Craig looked at the pistol as if he was thinking about going for it.

“I wouldn’t do that. You will be dead before your hand reaches it.”

“Maybe, maybe not,” he replied.

“No Craig, there is not a maybe. You will be dead. There are four guns aimed at you. If you even twitch, you will be dead.”

I could see a look of resignation come over him as he slumped in the wheel chair.

“Okay Craig, Wren, whatever the hell your name is, take your left hand, pick up the gun by the barrel and drop it on the floor. After the gun was on the floor, Sanchez and I entered and cuffed his hands in front of him. We put Craig in the cruiser and headed back to Ironton. On the way back I asked him, “How long you been in the wheel chair?”

“About a year and a half.”

“What happened,” I asked?

“Car wreck, paralyzed from the waist down

I would have to check his story and if it was true, that would eliminate him as a suspect in Don’s murder. When we got back to Ironton, we checked the reports for car accidents in the last year and a half. After an hour of checking, Sanchez came up with the report. It was a side hit and said the driver appeared to be paralyzed from the waist down. A call to the hospital confirmed the prognosis, so Sanchez called the Huntington PD and told them to start extradition proceedings on Marvin Wren/Winton Craig. While all this was going on I was interviewing Wren and the last Question I asked him. “Why didn’t you try to get out of the country?”

His reply, “Where better to hide than right under their noses.”

Chapter 14

I picked Rebecca up at the appointed time. She had on a black dress that fit her curves to a tee. Her blonde hair framed her beautiful face and her luscious red lips were enticing. With Rebecca on my arm, we walked out to the car and headed for the Latin Quarter. The wine was good, the food was great and the company was excellent. Around 10:00 o'clock, Rebecca suggested we leave and we headed back to her apartment. In her apartment, we sat on the couch and started touching each other. Her hands traced lines on my face and started down my torso, caressing my chest and stomach. As she unbuttoned my pants, I raised my hips off the couch. As my clothes were coming off, one by one, I was twisting and tugging at my shirt. Rebecca started kissing and licking my torso and when she encircled me, I thought I would go insane from the pleasure.

I pulled Rebecca up and had her stand in front of me. I stood, walked around her and slowly slipped the straps off her shoulders. I kissed the nape of her neck and let my hands slide slowly over her shapely body. Sliding the zipper down allowed her dress to fall at her feet. She kicked the dress to one side and stepped out of her shoes. As I rolled her hose down her legs, my lips were busy kissing her back and legs. Standing, I unhooked her bra and let my hands slide around and tease her breasts. Sliding my hands down her body, I hooked my fingers in her panties and slowly slid them down her legs. Turning her around, I directed my attention to her breasts. When my lips encircled one nipple then the other, Rebecca started sinking to the floor. By the time my lips touched her secret spot, she was laying on the floor. I rose above her and entered her feminine core. Every time I pushed into her, she would raise her hips and meet me. After what seemed like an eternity of passion, we collapsed in a tangle of arms and legs. After we lay there for a while, we got up and walked hand in hand to the bedroom. The second time making love also ended in a tangle of arms and legs. The sun was almost up when we arose and after a hearty breakfast I headed back to my apartment.

Chapter 15

Monday morning, I headed for the office and met Grady, Dickerson and Sanchez. We had the description of the killer and Sanchez had called a local artist to come to sketch Grady and make the changes to the sketch. When those changes were finished, we had a better image of the killer. After the artist was finished, I took the sketch back to the restaurant.

Rebecca said, “That’s him.”

Now all we had to do was find him.

One thing bothered me about the whole deal; the wolf’s head tattoo on the guys arm. I kept wondering if the tattoo had anything to do with Los Lobos and I had to find out. I told Sanchez and Dickerson about my gut feeling and told them I was going to Columbus to see the Doctor treating Eddie Crane. I wanted to see the wolf’s head tattooed on Eddie’s arm. Sanchez told me he’d have Grady check on Tim Ebbert and a few of the other boys that used to belong to the club. When I got to Columbus, I talked to Dr. Nichols. He was the shrink taking care of Eddie. He agreed to let me observe Eddie, but I could not talk to him or let him see me. The Doctor said Eddie was making progress and seeing me might set him back many months. After a few minutes of observing Eddie through a one way glass, I noticed a large scar on his right arm. "Doctor Nichols, why does Eddie have that large scar on his right arm.?"

"Well Mr. Stevens, Eddie had a large tattoo of some sort on his arm when he was admitted. The original Doctor, who admitted Eddie, said the day he came in, Eddie had eaten supper and evidently pocketed a fork. When they checked him the next morning, his arm was bleeding and the tattoo had been scraped off."

"Do you know what the tattoo was?"

"No I don't,"

"Will you ask the original Doctor what it was?"

"I'm sorry, he died a couple of months ago of a massive heart attack. I guess the stress of the job got to him."

"One more question. Can you ask your staff if any of them remembers what the tattoo was?"

"I'll see what I can find out."

"Thank you Doctor Nichols. If you find out, please call me at this number and let me know."

I handed him my card and headed back home.

Back in Ironton, I found out that Grady didn't have much luck either. I told Grady I thought the killer was connected to Los Lobos. I didn't know how, but my gut feeling was it was too much coincidence not to be related. Grady told me he would check out the tattoo parlor in Ashland and I could check out the parlors in Greenup and

Russell, Kentucky. Thursday morning, I drove across the bridge to Russell, Kentucky. Being the only tattoo parlor in Russell, it was not hard to find. I walked in and told the owner, covered with garish tattoos from his finger tips to his shoulders,

"I need a wolf head tattoo on my right forearm."

He replied, "I don't do wolf heads. It's too hard to get them realistic. There's an artist in Greenup and one in Kenova, West Virginia that does them. That's the only two I know of in the tri state area."

"Thanks, I'll check them out."

After I drove to Greenup, I asked around and got directions to the tattoo parlor.

After entering the shop, I looked around and pulled a picture of a wolf head off the wall.

"How much for this one?"

"Sorry buddy, that one is not for sale."

"Why" I asked?

"That one is special, only a few people can wear that one."

Again, I asked, "Why?"

"Because I said so, now put it back."

"Okay," I replied as I walked over to his wall of pictures and re-hung it. As I walked back to the counter desk, I removed my Federal ID and told him.

"I want to know why that design is special. We can talk now or you can accompany me to the station. It's up to you pal."

He became highly upset and told me, "You can't come in here making demands. This is my place of business, get the hell out."

"Okay pal." I said as I reached across the desk and snapped a cuff to his right arm. He started to struggle until I put a 38 special between his eyes. He stuttered and stammered until he was able to say,

"Easy with that damn thing, it may go off."

"Listen pal, I don't give a rat's ass if it does go off. You're resisting arrest and I can shoot you, put a piece in you hand and tell them it was self defense. You won't be around to dispute it, so who do you think the cops are going to believe. I had a partner killed by someone with a wolf head tattoo. He was shot in the back of the head and then they ripped out his throat. Now you can tell why that tattoo is so special or we are going to go a round or two. You got that?"

"Yeah, I got it. Just don't get excited and cut loose with that pistol."

"Okay, talk to me."

"Some dude came in about a year ago and gave me the design. He paid me a thousand dollars to keep it special. Only a few were allowed to have it."

"Who decided the people that were allowed to have the tattoo?"

"He did."

"How did you know when to use it?"

"He'd call me and give me a number. When his person

came in, they were supposed to give me the same number."

"What was the number?"

"It was supposed to change for every job."

"Have you received any calls from him lately?"

"No."

"When was the last time you used that design?"

"About five months ago; some young kid from Ohio. He paid me the hundred bucks and left."

"Did this kid have a name?"

"I'm sure he did but he never told me. He just gave me the number, I did the tattoo, he paid me the hundred bucks and left."

"If I come back tomorrow with a few pictures, do you think you can pick him out?"

"Maybe, but it's been five months and they all look alike to me."

"Well, for your sake, I hope you can."

"One more thing, if you run on me, I'll hunt you to the ends of the earth. You'll spend the rest of your life looking over your shoulder, wondering if I'm back there, and someday I will be."

"Hey man, I don't want any trouble. I'll be here tomorrow, just bring the damn pictures and I'll do my best."

"While you are being cooperative, if that Dude calls, give me call, if you know what's good for you."

"Okay," he meekly said.

Back in Ironton, I reported my findings to Sanchez and Dickerson. They agreed, while it was a step in the right direction, we still had a puzzler on our hands. Grady showed up around 2:00 o'clock and said just about the same results as I reported. Grady wasn't as nice as I was. He said he had to slap the guy around a bit when he tried to run. The guy thought Grady was sent in by his ex-wife to collect alimony and back child support. Grady was able to elicit one more bit of information from the Kenova location. The Dude had an Ohio tag on his car. From the description given Grady, the Dude seemed to be the same person in both cases.

Grady and I spent the rest of the day going through Don's patrol car and his desk in the squad room. We had to find out if Don was working on anything that might have gotten him killed. I searched the desk and found nothing but routine police matters. Grady didn't have any better luck with the patrol car until he went through Don's ticket book. There were two traffic stops that night. Grady brought the tickets in and asked Sanchez to run the plates on the two Ohio cars, which later turned out to be fruitless. He went back out to the car to continue his search. In about fifteen minutes, he returned with a slip of paper. On the paper, in Don's handwriting, were the words, Los Lobos. We had to find out if this was a recent note or something from several months ago.

Sanchez, Dickerson, Grady and I sat at the conference table in the squad room trying to come up with our next step. First of all, we needed to talk to Don's wife to see if he confided in her. Second, I need to get a picture of Eddie Crane to the tattoo shop in Greenup. Third, we needed to get a search warrant for the Crane house. I was hoping Eddie left some clues there. When we found the wolf suit several months ago, we stopped searching. And fourth, we need to get a warrant for the phone records at the tattoo parlors, plus we need to get the wolf head tattoo out to other police departments.

I took a picture of Eddie Crane, threw in a couple of others and headed for the Greenup Tattoo Parlor. Chopper, the owner, looked at the pictures for several minutes. I could tell he was stalling so I reached for my handcuffs. When he noticed them in my hands, he said, "Christ man, why you got to flash them things? I'm trying to remember who the kid was."

"Chopper, I think you're stalling. I saw a look of recognition cross you face when you looked at one of the pictures. You didn't hide your reaction very well. I'm asking you right now, you don't want me angry at you, do you?"

"No dammit, I'm trying to remember. Just give me a few more minutes, okay?""Sorry, your time is up. I'm kind of antsy right now. I wouldn't be surprised if you called the Dude when you saw me pull up. He or one of his cronies is probably on the way and you're trying to stall me until he gets here. Let me promise you this, if someone comes busting through that door, you will be the first to die. You got that, Chopper?"

"Yeah, I got it. Here, it was this kid?"

"Chopper, you're a lying son of a bitch. That kid is a cop. You got five seconds to tell me the truth. Five—Four—Three—"

"Okay, okay, it was this kid."

"What's his name?"

"All I know is Eddie something."

"Very good Chopper, now you get to live a little longer. I think I'll stick around a while anyway. Hell, I might even get a tattoo. How much would you charge me?"

"I ain't doing anything for you. Just get the hell out of my shop."

"You act like you're anxious for me to leave, Chopper. You got somebody out there waiting for me to come out. Maybe, I'll let you wear my shirt and let you walk out. With all those tattoos covered up, a person would have a hard time telling it was you walking out instead of me. What do you think about that Chopper?"

"I ain't going out that door. You're fucking crazy if you think I'm going out there."

"That's what I thought; give me your damn phone." When I dialed the Ironton PD, Chopper said, ""Hey asshole, you can't use my phone to call long distance."

"No problem," I said, "If you don't want me to use the phone, you walk out the front door."

"Go ahead, use the damn phone," he replied.

"Sanchez, this is Jack. I need back up at the Greenup Tattoo Parlor. I think someone is outside waiting to shoot me when I come out."

"Okay Jack, I'll call Chief Reynolds at Greenup PD. He should be able to have someone there in a few minutes."

"Thanks Juan, I'm bringing this asshole in on a federal arrest. I think he knows more than he's telling. Is Grady back from talking to Don's wife?"

"Not yet Jack, but he is due back soon."

"Ask him if he'll stick around a few minutes, I want to know what he found out."

Chapter 16

Grady pulled up in front of Don's house. Mrs. Hamilton answered the door and it looked like she had been crying. "Mrs. Hamilton, I'm Grady Hicks. I was Don's partner for a while and I know it's a bad time to be asking questions, but I need to ask a few, if you're up to it?"

"I'll try to answer your questions," she replied.

"Did Don ever confide in you about what he was working on?"

"Sometimes, he would. He usually told me about the arrests he made. He was proud to be a cop and felt he could make a difference. He mentioned your name a few times, Mr. Hicks"

"Please, call me Grady. Did Don ever mention anything about a club or gang that might be involved in something criminal?"

"About a week before he was killed, he mentioned something about meeting a person who might be able to fill him in on some sort of gang activity."

"Did he say who he was meeting?"

"No, he just said it would be in the next week or so. Don wanted to move up in the police department and he thought the information could give him the break he was looking for."

"Did he say where this meeting was supposed to take place?"

"All he told me was it was supposed to take place at some restaurant."

"Mrs. Hamilton, did Don keep any police business or paper work at home?"

"We have..., I mean, I have a den where he used to spend time after getting off work. It's so hard to remember Don is no longer here. I miss him terribly."

"May I look around in the den? There may be something there that will help us find his killer."

"By all means, go ahead," she replied. Grady searched everything in the den and was getting ready to leave. On a whim, he lifted the desk blotter and there taped to the bottom of the blotter was a slip of paper with the words, Los Lobos and Moores, written on it. The paper matched the type of paper that Don carried in his patrol car.

"Mrs. Hamilton, did Don ever say anything to you about Los Lobos?"

"No Grady. Do you think it had anything to do with his death?"

"I don't know yet, but it's an angle we're pursuing. We'll let you know if anything comes of it. My own personal gut feeling is that it is connected. All we have to do is find that connection."

Chapter 17

The Greenup Police came screaming up and slid to a stop in front of the tattoo parlor. Chief Reynolds was the first officer in the building and demanded to know who I was. I introduced my self and showed him my ID. "I need Chopper held for a few days. He's a material witness in an attempted murder and might even be an accessory to murder."

"Who's the attempted murder?"

"Mine," I replied. "There was someone outside waiting for me to come out of the building. I think Chopper called them when I pulled up a little while ago."

The Chief said, "Must have been the car that pulled out when we came screaming up."

"Did you get a look at it?" I asked.

"Yeah, a white 62 Chevy Impala, four door."

"Did you happen to get a license number?"

"No, after Sanchez called, we rolled like a bat out of hell."

"That's okay, we'll get him eventually. Hold Chopper for a few days. I'll be back in a day or so to talk to him again."

Back in Ironton, I filled Sanchez and Dickerson in on

the action in Greenup. Grady came in about twenty minutes later and told us how the interview went with Mrs. Hamilton. "You know guys," he said, "I don't know how but this whole deal is tied into Los Lobos. I think we need to send out some inquiries to the surrounding states to see if any of them know anything about Los Lobos. In the meantime, let's make the plans to serve the search warrant for the Crane house. Maybe we stopped to soon the last time. While we're at it, let's see if we can get one for Choppers tattoo parlor, his house and try for one at the tattoo parlor in Kenova."

Dickerson said he would re-send a copy of the tattoo to all the surrounding police departments.

Monday morning, the sun was shining brightly and Don's funeral was scheduled for 11:00 AM. There were representatives from every police department within a hundred miles of Ironton. The Police Honor Guard led the procession from the funeral home to the cemetery. Don's patrol car was second in line and the hearse carrying Don's body was third in line. His patrol car had a black banner stretched across each front door and the Honor Guard wore black strips across their badges. Mrs. Hamilton, along with Sanchez and Dickerson, rode in the family car behind the hearse. Six police officers, in dress blues, carried the casket to the grave site. After the casket was placed on the bier, every officer saluted as a 21 gun salute was fired over Don's grave.

The police Chaplain, David Sedgewick, delivered the

final comments at the grave. Don's wife, openly sobbing, received the flag from the casket. As she arose to leave, she stepped forward and kissed the casket, removed one red rose from the bouquet and held it to her bosom. Sanchez and Dickerson helped her back to the family car. After the mourners dispersed, Grady and I were the only ones left standing there. Just before the funeral director lowered the casket into the ground, we walked up and both of us placed a hand on the casket. "Good-bye old friend. You will be missed. Your death will be avenged and retribution will be terrible."

Grady affirmed the oath with, "Amen."

We withdrew our hands and gave one final salute to our brother in arms. As the funeral director released the catch, Don's casket slowly disappeared into the cool dark earth. Grady followed suit as I walked over and picked up a handful of earth. Walking back to Don's slowly descending casket, we let the earth fall on the casket.

Grady spoke, "You will be avenged."

"Amen." I replied.

When I reported in Tuesday morning, Dickerson handed me a search warrant for the Crane house. Grady, two other officers, and I were standing on the porch at 9:00 AM. Mr. Crane was visibly upset when he answered the door and I showed him the search warrant. "You people are not coming in here again. You're the damn reason Eddie is in the crazy house."

"No sir," I replied. "You're the reason he's there. You

tried to be a buddy to Eddie when you should have been a father. He used your gun to shoot that woman and he needed a father all these years, since your wife died, not a buddy. I'm coming in there if I have to whip you ass to do it and after I whip your ass, you're going to jail. I'll charge you with so much, you'll be lucky if you get out in six years. Now what's it going to be?"

"Go ahead, search the damn place, but don't expect me to help."

We started in the kitchen. The stove, refrigerator, the cabinets and the pantry were thoroughly searched. We left nothing unturned. The living room, bathroom, bedrooms, and the attic were all gone over with a fine tooth comb. We weren't having any luck and Mr. Crane was becoming a pain in the rear. Twice, Grady had to tell him to back off or he was going to take his ass to jail. We had the basement and the garage to search. We were just about finished with the basement when I took a breather. Sitting on a box, I noticed a vent overhead. Something seemed odd about it. It took me a minute to notice the difference in the screws holding the vent to the duct work. The ductwork had been painted white and two of the screws had the paint missing from the screwdriver slot.

"Conahan, bring me a regular screwdriver."

He looked around for a minute and brought one over to me. "Here you go, Jack."

When I removed the screws, the vent dropped down a few inches. I removed the remaining screws and took the vent down. Reaching up inside the ductwork, I felt something metal. When I removed it, it had three metal claws extending from some sort of a glove. Each claw had a serrated edge about an inch long. Feeling around in the duct, produced another claw. One for each hand, I thought.

"Mr. Crane, come down here, please." After he was in the basement, I asked. "What are these?"

"I don't know," he replied. "I've never seen them before."

"Let me tell you what they are. They are slipped on someone's hands and used to rip out a person's throat, just like Don Hamilton several days ago."

"I didn't know anything about them," he whined, "Honest to God."

"You know what I think," I replied, "These are yours or Eddie's and they were used to kill Don and since Eddie is in the state hospital they must be yours. We're taking these as evidence and I'm going to have them tested for blood residue. If it matches Don's blood type, you're going up for murder."

Grady snapped the cuffs on him and we locked the house and headed downtown.

After booking Crane for suspicion of murder, Sanchez had an officer dust the claws for prints. There were two sets of prints, mine and Eddies. When we finished with the prints, I took the claws to the coroner's office. When I walked in, I asked George to check them for blood residue and if so, let me know the type. George came back a little later and told me, "There's no human blood residue, but there are traces of animal blood. Where in the hell did you get these things?"

"We found them at Eddie Crane's house. Could they have been used to rip out Don's throat?"

George looked them over real good and told me,

"The blades of these are compatible with the wounds on Don's throat. They are not the ones used but I bet they are similar to what was used on Don."

I went back to the office and told Sanchez and Dickerson what George said. About a half hour later I heard a commotion from the front of the station. Mr. James Kelly, Crane's lawyer was raising hell with the desk sergeant. Mr. Kelly had been around town for a long time and was a real sleaze ball. Even though I didn't like him, he would be my first choice if I were in a tight spot. I walked out to the desk and told Kelly to shut the hell up.

"I will when I get to see my client." I went back to see Sanchez and told him, "Turn Crane loose. He isn't the one we're after."

After Crane was released, he came by the duty desk and started raising hell with me.

"Stevens, I'm going to sue you and whole police department."

"Listen asshole, you better get out of here while you can still walk under you own power."

"Is that a threat?" he asked.

"You're damn straight it is. Now get out of my face. What

you let your son get into was a tragedy. That boy started turning bad a long time ago and you ignored him. Now, get out of here before I throw your ass in jail for being a jerk and take your damn Lawyer with you before I arrest him for being a damn jerk, too. Now get out of my sight."

Sanchez looked at me like I was crazy. "You were a little hard on them boys, weren't you Jack?"

"Hell no, they both deserve to be arrested for being jerks."

Grady spoke up, "Come on guys, we don't need any dissension among the troops. We got work to do."

"Okay, I'm sorry I snapped at you Juan. I'm frustrated as hell because we don't have anything."

Chapter 18

"Since Grady is still in charge of this investigation, with his permission, there are a couple more things we need to do. We need to stake out the Kenova tattoo shop and we need to pick up the warrants to get his phone records. What do you think Grady?"

"One other thing, we need make sure all the flyers went out and double check to see if we got any hits"

"Okay Grady, what do you need me to do?"

"Jack. I need you to take a couple of guys to Chopper's shop and go through it with a fine tooth comb. Pay attention to bills, especially phone bills. Bring back whatever you find that may be of help. I'll take a couple of guys and search his home and we need a couple of guys to stake out the Kenova tattoo parlor."

Dickerson spoke up, "You guys are crossing state lines. Let me supply a couple of my guys for each of you. We can't have local cops crossing state lines. Jack, you'll be okay by yourself because you're still deputized but let me supply a couple of guys to help in the search. Grady, you'll need a couple of my guys to carry this off. I'll make sure they know you're in charge. Meet me back here in an hour and then you can go after whatever you need." An hour later, we were all on our way to do a little hunting.

After going through the tattoo parlor, I only found one phone bill. It had not been paid and one of the numbers caught my eye. It was to Cincinnati, Ohio and it was the day I went to Choppers with the picture of Eddie Crane. After we finished and locked the shop, we went out to help Grady do Chopper's house. Grady said he found several phone bills and as we compared the numbers, there were three calls to the same number in Cincinnati. Back at the station, Sanchez picked up the phone and called the number. A female answered, "Three R Corporation."

Sanchez told her, "I'm sorry, I think I got the wrong number."

"Who were you trying to get in touch with sir?" she asked

"The Turner Corporation," replied Juan.

"I'm sorry sir you reached the Three R Corporation."

"Excuse me, have a good day." Juan said as he hung up the phone.

"Jack, can you go to Cincinnati and do a little research on the Three R Corporation?"

"Sure," I replied, "I'll leave in the morning."

Thursday was a nice day so I fired up the beast and rode to Cincinnati, arriving around noon and immediately found a pay phone. When I made the call, the phone was answered as The Three R Corporation.

"I'm sorry," I said, "I must have dialed the number wrong."

Rose Holden, the receptionist at the Three R Corporation, entered the back room and told her brother, "Russ, that's the second wrong number in two days. I think we better move our operation to another location. The only people that knew our number were the tattoo parlors we gave it to. There is something fishy going on and I don't like it."

"Okay Rose, your instincts have always been good. We'll move to the training compound in Bainbridge. You start packing the records. Leave everything else. Don't worry about the office supplies and small stuff. We just need the records. I'll call the Captain and tell him to get a couple of rooms ready. We'll operate out of there for a while and if nothing comes of the phone calls, we'll move back in town. Remember, just the files. We can come back later for the other stuff."

My next step was to go through the phone book to see if The Three R Corporation was listed. That idea proved useless so I had to go straight to the phone company. After identifying myself as a Federal Agent and telling them I needed the address for that phone number, a Mr. Collins refused to reveal the address to me. "Mr. Collins, why are you being so difficult? You know I can get a court order to get the address. Why don't you save me some time and yourself some trouble from my boss? He's a nasty SOB and I am asking politely." He finally caved in and asked his secretary to get the address for me. When she returned, she handed me a skip of paper with address written on it, 1301 Third Street., cross street is Erkenberger, near the zoo.

"Thank you," I replied.

After asking directions, I rode over to Third Street. When I finally found the building it was an old block building that looked like it had been used as an auto shop of some sort. An old oil sign was attached to the front of the building, along with a spark plug sign. Four roll up doors fronted the building and there was an old "H" hoist to the left side of the building. On the right side of the building were stairs leading to the second floor. Shutting off the beast, I walked across the littered parking lot to the stairs. As I started up the stairs, I noticed the door was slightly open. Easing up the stairs, I stopped at the top when I heard a sound that sounded like desk drawers being opened and closed. Pushing the door open a little more, I saw a man rifling through the desk drawers. He appeared to be in his fifties and wasn't dressed very well. Pulling my weapon as I kicked the door open, I jumped in the room and told him, "Freeze, Police."

Immediately his hands were up over his head. "I didn't break in. I saw a couple of people leave with a few boxes. The lady told the guy she forgot to close the door. He told her to forget about it. I was setting under the steps and when they left, I waited a while to make sure they were gone then I came up to see if there was anything I could pawn."

"What's your name?" I asked.

"Ezra, Ezra Hopkins."

"How long ago did they leave?"

"About two hours ago."

"Which way did they go?"

"North on Third Street."

"What kind of car did they have?"

"A white four door Chevy."

"Ezra, did you take anything?"

"No sir. I was just looking around for a few things to sell so I could get something to eat."

"Okay Ezra, here is twenty bucks. Go get something to eat. Oh, did you happen to see them?"

"No sir, like I said, I was under the steps. Just heard them talking."

After Ezra left, I looked around a bit. The only things I could find were office supplies, an old desk and an empty filing cabinet. All the paper work was missing from the filing cabinet. I started to call Dickerson from the desk phone but changed my mind. There were probably finger prints on there so I closed the door and walked down the stairs to find a pay phone.

"Dickerson, I found the address for the Three R Corporation. It's 1301 Third Street. Can you get a finger print team in here? The place was vacated in a hurry, about two hours ago. There's no paper in the office but they left some equipment we might be able to lift prints off."

"Okay Jack, I have a team across the river in Covington, I'll get them over there. May take an hour or so, but I'll get them there as quick as possible."

"Thanks. I'm going back up to the building. There are a lot of bums around here. Since the building is not locked, I need to make sure no one goes in and destroys evidence. I'll wait until the team gets here."

I sat in front of the building and around 7:00 PM a car pulled up. Two men got out, carrying cases, and walked towards me. "You Jack?"

"Yeah."

"We're Henderson and McGowan. Dickerson sent us to dust for prints. Is this the building?"

"Yes, up the stairs to the right. I'll stick around until you guys get finished.

"We'll be a couple of hours."

"I'll be here."

When they came back down, the said they got several prints in the receptionist area and three in the back office. We'll run them through our system and give Dickerson a call if we get a match."

Back in Ironton, I learned Grady was still on stake out at the Kenova tattoo parlor. He had been there since Thursday morning. I drove up Friday morning to relieve him and he gave me a list of the license plate numbers of the clients frequenting the parlor. Most of the numbers were from Ohio and I figured they were not the person we were trying to find because the tag numbers were all local prefixes. Saturday morning, Grady and another local officer, Wayne Holt, relieved me. Grady told me,

"We'll stay until closing and follow the owner home. We might as well watch his home for the rest of the night."

Most businesses were closed on Sunday as the "Blue Law" was in effect. Most of the stores that were open on Sunday were gas stations and a few grocery stores.

Chapter 19

Russ Holden and his sister, Rose, pulled into the training camp around 2:00 PM on Thursday. The first thing they noticed, after the half mile long ride back the driveway was the wolf head mounted over the main gate to the compound. The Captain, Ron Holden, was surprised to see them so early. “I thought you’d still be packing.”

“We were,” replied Russ, “but Rose got an uneasy feeling this morning. After we called you, we just packed up the important papers and took off.”

“Well, I hope you didn’t leave any finger prints behind.”

Russ knew they did, but his brother would not like that, so he lied.

“We wiped everything off before we left.”

Rose was about to say something to the contrary. Ron’s head was turned away and Russ put his finger to his lips so Rose could see. Ron turned back to them and said,

“It’s best to pay attention to your instincts. That’s how I survive. I don’t ignore them.”

Russ asked if he could get a couple of recruits to help unload the car.

“Sure thing,” replied Ron. “Peterson, Adams, over here

on the double." They came running up, stood at attention, and saluted the Captain.

"Unload the car and put the boxes in cabin two."

"Yes sir," they replied, in unison.

As Peterson and Adams set about their chore, Russ, Ron, and Rose walked into Cabin 1, Ron's headquarters. Inside Ron asked Rose why she felt the need to run.

"First of all," she replied, "we had two wrong number calls, close together. Second we had a contractor that was supposed to take care of a problem. We tried to reach him after he was supposed to have the problem resolved and he wasn't at his usual post. Third, we couldn't get in touch with Chopper to see if the problem had been eliminated."

"Good job. Rose, you did the right thing. You guys hungry, the cook just finished feeding the troops and there should be enough left for the three of us. Come on; let's walk over to the mess tent."

On the way to the mess tent, they walked past four young men disassembling rifles.

Ron said, "Their job is to take them apart, clean them and put them back together. They will do this until they can do it with their eyes closed." Out to the left of the mess hall were six men practicing hand to hand combat. They were dressed in camo outfits and blended perfectly with the background. About that time a volley of shots rang out. Russ and Rose instinctively ducked and Ron just chuckled at them. "Easy guys, it's just a few recruits on the rifle range."

Inside the mess hall, two recruits were slaving over their KP duties. All three siblings sat and talked while the cook filled their plates. After eating Ron told them,

"Come on, I'll show you around. We've made a lot of changes since you were here the last time." Leaving the mess hall, they turned to the right. "This is our hand to hand station. The loser of each simulation gets three lashes for losing." He pointed at a bamboo pole and continued, "That gives them the incentive to be the winner."

Walking a little more, they came upon the shooting range. Four young men were practicing on silhouettes of human form. "Those high powered rifles are the best that money can buy," Ron said. "The scopes are ten power. A good man can drive a nail at a hundred yards."

Russ picked up a rifle and looked through the scope. Ninety per cent of the hits were head shots. Walking around a small mound of dirt put them in a wooded area.

Ron asked them, "Do you see anyone?"

Russ and Rose, both shook their heads. Ron blew a whistle and six young men stood up. Some were as close as twenty feet and had twigs and leaves all over their outfits.

The next area they encountered was fenced in. Ron told them, "This is our survival compound, fifty acres. The fence was put in years ago. When we bought it, we had to mend the fence in several areas. Couldn't have any one come in and do it, they might ask a lot of questions. Every recruit will spend a week in here with only a knife. He has to provide his own shelter and food. We only had two wash out. There buried over there," he said as he pointed to the graves.

Russ was amazed at the progress his big brother made at the camp. He felt confident that they were training the best damn assassins in the world and when they became known in the underworld, they would get rich in very short order. Ron had really thought of everything. When a new man was recruited, they would pick him up at a predetermined location, slip a black hood over his head and drive around for twenty four hours before bringing him to the camp. By then, the recruit was so disoriented; he had no idea where he was. Captain Holden taught each of his recruits to be proficient in the art of killing. Pistols, rifles, knives, hand to hand, bow and arrow, and the old fashioned methods such as garrote and poison were taught at the camp.

"You've done well, big brother." Russ said, "I'm impressed. It won't be long until we can put out the word for a few contracts."

"That's right," little brother, "It won't be long."

Rose was in awe of the operation. She knew it wouldn't be long until her brothers made her rich beyond her wildest dreams. She knew the whole operation. They would have to cut her in on the profit. Rose told them what she wanted to do.

"I want to go through the training. I'm getting tired of

being a secretary. You know there are places a woman can go without arousing suspicion and I know I'd be good at it."

"Okay little sister, you got a deal. The only place you can't go is the survival area. I brought wolves in from Montana and they're hungry all the time. They'd eat you alive. In fact, that's what happened to the two I buried. They didn't find a secure place to sleep. We had to take a party in to find them. The first one was probably killed the first night of two. There was nothing but bone left of him. When we stumbled on the second body, the wolves were still eating him. Did you see that wolf head over the gate? He was the alpha male and didn't want to give up his meal. He charged me and I had to shoot him. It really broke my heart to kill him, but he charged me and thought he could make me back down. That's when I had to drop him. All in all we have a good success rate and I have four fully trained assassins. I have four more that are about half way through the training."

Rose asked, "How long does it take to train?"

"About six months," replied Ron. "We're going to start another class in about three months. "We'll see about getting you started in that one. But in the meantime let me introduce you to our first graduate, Ralph Contee. Mr. Contee, front and center."

Chapter 20

Monday morning, Dickerson, Hicks, Sanchez and I met in Juan's office. We agreed we were at another stand still. We regrouped and Juan said he would take the Cincinnati Police and pursue the inquiry about Los Lobos. Dickerson volunteered to contact the two police departments that had not responded to the flyers he sent out. Grady agreed to take a stab at getting Eddie to talk since Dr. Nichols was not going to let me talk to him. I was left with Tim Ebbert. I cracked Tim once before. If I leaned on him, he might recall a little more than he's letting on.

In the afternoon, I drove to Tim's house and his Mother was out in the yard raking leaves. Tim was released early from juvenile hall for good behavior, but was still under house arrest for a few more weeks. He managed to complete his GED in juvenile hall and seem to be walking the straight and narrow.

"Hello Mr. Stevens, Tim is not in any more trouble, is he?"

"No Ma'am, I just need to talk to him."

Mrs. Ebbert went in the house and came back out with Tim.

"I didn't do anything. I've only been home for a couple of weeks and I spend all my time in the house."

"I know Tim. I'm not here to hassle you. I just need to talk to your for a few minutes, okay?"

"Yeah, I guess so. What do you want to talk about?"

"Eddie Crane," I replied.

"I told you everything I know about Eddie."

"I know that too, Tim, but there's things you may know about Eddie that you don't realize you know."

"Like what?"

"First of all, did Eddie ever say anything to you about the Three R Corporation?"

Tim stood there for a few minutes and I could just about see the gears working in his head.

"Now that you mention it, I did hear part of a conversation he had with some guy at the youth center. The guy mentioned Three R and then said something about training in a few months. When that guy left, I asked Eddie about it and he told me to forget about it. I didn't remember it until you mentioned it."

"Tim, try to remember, it's very important. Did you hear anything else?"

The gears were turning again as he wrinkled his brow.

"No, nothing else."

"Can you describe the other man?"

"He was an older man, about thirty, around 6' tall, dark hair and maybe 190 pounds. Oh yeah, I noticed a wolf head tattoo on his left arm, kind of like the one Eddie had."

"Are you sure it was a wolf tattoo?"

"Yeah, I saw Eddie's the day after he got it. The tattoo was just like Eddie's. I asked Eddie where he got it because I wanted one too. Eddie told me you got to earn it."

"Is there anything else you can tell me, Tim?"

"No, that's about it. If I remember anything, I'll call you."

I thanked Tim and his mother and turned to leave. Just as I reached my car, Tim said wait a minute, "I just thought of something else."

I walked back and asked, "What's that?"

"A few weeks after that I was dancing with Judy Rowan at the youth center and she asked me why Eddie was going to Cincinnati. Eddie never said anything to me about going away."

"Where does Miss Rowan live?"

"On Latonia Street, I think 816 Latonia."

"Thanks Tim, you've been a big help. I'll make sure your case worker hears of your help.

I called Dickerson and let him know what Tim said and I told him, "I'm going to see Miss Rowan. She may know more about Eddie Crane."

Mr. Rowan answered the door and I introduced myself and told him I needed to talk to Judy.

"What about?" he asked.

"Eddie Crane, I think Judy was friends with him at one time."

"Yes she was, until I ran him off. She came home one Friday night and told me he tried to get fresh with her on the dance floor. Eddie came around the following night and wanted her to go out with him. I told him if I ever saw him around my daughter again, I'd break his damn neck. She told me he never bothered her again." He turned and walked to the stairs, "Judy, honey come down here for a minute, please."

I heard a reply from upstairs, "Okay Daddy."

Judy was a beautiful young lady and she was going to break a lot of hearts before she got married.

"Judy, this is Jack Stevens, a Federal Agent. He's working with the Ohio State Police. He wants to ask you some questions about Eddie Crane."

"Eeww, that creep." she said

"Judy, Tim Ebbert said you asked him one night why Eddie was going to southwestern Ohio. Tim said he didn't know anything about it. Do you mind telling me what Eddie said to you?"

"I was dancing one night with Eddie, at the youth center, and he told me he was going to be gone for six months. I ask him why and he said he was going to take some military training. I asked him if he was going into the army and he said no. Then I asked him why are you going. He said he was training to be an assassin. Yeah right, I told him, I'm going to be the Easter Bunny. He told me, you'll see after Mr. Holton, or something like that, trains me. I told him, I'd heard the wind blow before. While we were dancing, he tried to feel my breasts and I walked away from him. He showed up at our house the next night and Daddy ran him off. I never saw him after that and forgot about him until I read in the paper where he killed those people"

"Judy, think real hard. The name he mentioned. What was it?"

"It was kind of noisy, with the juke box playing, but I thought it was Holton, or something like that. Like I said, it was noisy."

"Judy, could it have been Holland or something else?"

"No. it was an HO sound, I remember that much for sure."

"Did Eddie say anything else about the training he was supposed to take?"

"No, after he got fresh, I never talked to him anymore."

Back at the station, I filled the guys in on what Judy told me.

Chapter 21

Grady was back in town on Thursday and didn't have any luck in Cincinnati. Dickerson's inquiries to the two police departments did not produce any results. We were at a standstill again except for the idea of a training camp somewhere in South Western Ohio. That would cover an area from Columbus west to the state line and south to the Ohio River. That was an extremely large area and probably encompassed several thousand square miles. We spent the several days going back over what we had. Tim and the other boys in the club were interviewed again. We even re-interviewed the relatives of Eddie's victims. We just could not find that single thread that would unravel the whole deal. Every day, I thought of Don, what he looked like before and after. I could not give up. Somewhere there was a clue that would help solve the case. Another two weeks passed and we were still running around in circles.

I received a call from Dickerson at 4:00 AM on Sunday. "Jack, meet me at the station as soon as possible. I've called Grady and Sanchez."

"What's up?" I asked.

"Another assassination like Don's," Dickerson replied.

"Who?" I asked.

"I'll tell you when you get here."

I hurriedly dressed and was at the station by 4:20. Sanchez and Dickerson were already there and Grady was just a few steps behind me.

"Jack, what's up?"

"I don't know, I just got a call from Dickerson and he said to get here quick. He said there was another assassination like Don's."

"Do you know who?"

"I don't know. He said he'd tell us when we got here."

The mood in the briefing room was somber. Dickerson was drumming his finger tips on the table and Sanchez was rolling a pencil from hand to hand. Dickerson acknowledged us as we entered. "Sit down guys. We had an incident last night in Cincinnati. Senator Jason Hartley was assassinated. Same MO as Don Hamilton. Shot in the back of the head and his throat was ripped out."

I spoke up, "Did they catch anyone?"

"No," replied Dickerson, "It wasn't discovered until around midnight. The Senator was supposed to catch a red eye flight back to Washington at 2:00 AM. His aide said the Senator went to his room around 11:00 o'clock in the Park Lane Hotel to get his baggage. When he hadn't come back down by 11:45, the aide went up to see what was keeping him. That's when he discovered the body."

"Did any of the guests hear or see anything?"

"One lady, Mrs. Andrew Simpson was going to her room and said she rode up the elevator with the Senator. She said she watched the Senator enter his room and that no one else was in the hall. There are no suspects that we know of. Jack, I want you and Grady to take off for Cincinnati this morning. We're going to get some heat from this one. Grady, you have just been deputized a Federal Agent."

Grady and I left for Cincinnati around 6:00 AM and arrived at the Park Lane Hotel at 9:00 o'clock. We introduced ourselves to the Captain in charge, J.D. Ernst.

"Captain, we're not here to interfere with your investigation. We're here to help. We had a similar MO on a homicide a while back and we want to see if you, or we, can make a connection between the two murders. He looked us over carefully and finally said.

"Okay guys, this one is especially brutal and we should work together to get this bastard. He may be the same one that did your guy."

"Great Captain, we'll do whatever we can to help. What would you like for us to do?"

"I need help interviewing all the guests. Most of them are still here. A few have insisted they have to leave this afternoon to get back to work by tomorrow morning. Those individuals are the ones we would like to talk to first. Can you and Grady take those for us?"

Grady and I took a list of twelve individuals. Six of them were in their rooms before 10:00 PM and two did not return to their rooms until after 2:00AM. The four left returned during the time period of 10:00 PM and midnight. They were the ones we spent the most time with. Even so, they really didn't know anything. We returned to Captain Ernst, around 12:00 Noon and told him we drew a blank. He asked, "Jack, can you and Grady help interview the evening shift. They come on a 3:00 o'clock?"

"We'll be glad to Captain. Since we missed breakfast, is there someplace close we can grab a bite to eat?"

"Sure thing," he replied, "Lou's Deli, out the door, turn right and go around the corner. It's a good place to eat."

"Thanks," we chipped in.

We sat at small table and started talking about the case. One other customer, a good looking redhead was seated near us. I kept sneaking looks at her. It had been a long time since I had seen someone like her, hair just below the shoulder, emerald green eyes, and a complexion like peaches and cream. She caught me looking once and a smile lit up her face. When she smiled, there was a twinkle in her eyes that suggested a mischievous streak might be hiding behind those green eyes. As Grady and I continued to talk, she got up, walked over and pulled out a chair at our table. "You guys cops?" she asked.

"Matter of fact, we are."

"What are your names? I haven't seen you around here before."

"That's because we're not from around here."

"Where you from?" she asked

"Why do you want to know?"

"Because I'm a reporter for the City Examiner. I'm Marlo Huston."

"I'm Jack Stevens and this is Grady Hicks. We're Federal Agents."

Are you guys working on the Senator's killing?"

"We're helping," I replied.

I don't know why but something, other than hormones, told me this lady was okay.

"Marlo, since we are new to the area, I may need information and you can supply that. I may need help on certain people and as a reporter, again, you can help. If you help me, I'll see that you get any information I have, exclusively."

"Now, I told you what we are doing here. What brought you out?"

"I was covering the Senators speech last night and I had a gut feeling to follow him back to the hotel. After he went in the hotel, around 11:00 o'clock last night, I decided to head home. Just as I was walking to my car, I saw a man walking up the hotel drive with a box under his arm. It looked like a box of flowers and I wondered why he didn't drive up to the door, like all the other flower deliveries. I thought it was strange and decided to hang around a little longer. About twenty minutes later, I saw him walking back down the drive without the box and he just walked off into the night."

"Did you tell this to the police?"

“Yes, some cop told me that there was a flower delivery to a couple who just got married at the hotel. When I asked him about the flowers, he said the flowers were delivered and the delivery person took the box out to the trash. I looked in the dumpster this morning and there was a flower box in there but it was not the one I saw last night”

“Did you get a good look at this person?”

“Yes,” she replied.

“What did he look like?”

Marlo described him as 6’ tall, 180 pounds, blond hair, and a ruddy complexion. “Oh yeah,” she said, “He had a wolf head tattoo on his left forearm.”

Bells went off in my head and I asked her, “Did the delivery man see you?”

“Yes.”

“Did he get a good enough look to identify you?”

“Probably,” she said. “Why?”

“Marlo, these people are professionals and they won’t leave anyone alive that can identify them. You’re going to have to be very careful.”

Chapter 22

Ralph Contee was the first graduate of the training camp. Captain Holden said he was the best he had ever trained. Ralph was going to prove the Captain right. Tonight he would assassinate Senator Jason Hartly. Ralph had a very narrow window of opportunity as the Senator was flying back to DC tonight after his speech at an Anti Defamation League Conference. Ralph would have to complete this assignment without being seen.

Ralph knocked on the door of Riverside Florists a little after 5:00 PM.

"Sorry sir, we're closed," came a reply from the other side of the drawn door shade.

"Please Ma'am, I got stuck in traffic. I really tried to get here in time. I have a friend getting married in less than an hour and I promised I'd pick up a dozen red roses for his new bride. I'll make it worthwhile if you'll just open up for a few minutes, plus you'll make a new bride and groom very happy"

"Okay, just a minute." The clerk unlocked the door and Ralph stepped inside.

"I really appreciate this and I know the bride and groom

will be very happy. She wrapped a dozen red roses, put them in a box, and handed them to Ralph.

"That will be thirty dollars," she said.

"Here's a fifty, keep the change."

As she turned towards the register, Ralph pulled out his silenced 45 pistol and shot her in the back of the head. He thought about ripping out her throat but that would put to much heat on him. Two in the same night would be more than coincidence. Stepping around the counter, he emptied the register and pulled her body back a few feet so it wouldn't be seen from the sidewalk. Tucking the flowers under his arm, he turned out the light; made sure the lock was set, and walked out the door. The police will chalk this up to a botched robbery, he mused to himself.

Since he had several hours to kill, he drove to Covington, Kentucky and had supper. Around 9:00 PM, he made his way to the Park Lane Hotel and waited for the Senator to arrive. When the Senator's car arrived at the hotel, Ralph got out of his car and started walking towards the hotel. As he walked up the ramp, he passed a young lady walking out. He thought about shooting her on the spot but she was still in the lights of the hotel and that would jeopardize his mission. He took a good look at her so he could find her later and kill her. Ralph called earlier and finagled the Senator's room number by pretending to be a reporter.

When Contee approached the front door of the hotel, he stopped and looked in the window. The lobby was empty and the desk clerk was not behind the reception desk. "Perfect," he muttered as he stepped in the front door. Scurrying past the desk, he had another hundred feet to get to the stair well. Reaching the stair well, without being seen, he started up the stairs to the tenth floor. After throwing the flowers in a trash can on the third floor, he continued to the eighth floor and deposited the empty box in a trash can in the stair well. He continued on to the tenth floor stair well, and eased out the door into the hall. Good, he thought, no one around and he cautiously walked down the hall to room 1005, knocking on the door, he heard a reply from the Senator, "Who is it?"

"Bell Boy," was the reply, "here to take you luggage down."

"Okay, just a minute." A few seconds later, the Senator opened the door and turned to walk back in the room. The Senator took four steps and Ralph Contee was right behind him. Ralph pulled the trigger on his 45 and Senator Jason Hartly was dead before he hit the floor.

"Well, Well, Senator Hartly, this next part is the one I really enjoy." Ralph pulled the claws from a leather pouch and proceeded to rip out the Senator's throat.

Ralph Contee reversed his steps and got out of the hotel the same way he got in, unseen. Walking back down the ramp, he noticed the young lady sitting in a vehicle by the curb. There were people coming out of the hotel and he was afraid to risk shooting her. As he walked past, he turned and looked at the license plate number. That number was burned into his memory.

Back at the training compound, Ralph reported in to Captain Holden.

“How did it go, Mr. Contee?”

“Mission accomplished, Sir.”

“Any problems, Mr. Contee?”

“Just one Sir.”

“And what was that, Mr. Contee?”

“There was a woman walking out and I think she got a good look at me, Sir.”

“Did you eliminate her?”

“No Sir.”

“Why not, Mr. Contee?”

“There were cars going by and people coming out of the hotel, Sir.”

“That is not an excuse, Mr. Contee.”

“I know Sir, but I got the license plate number of her car. It’s a detail I will take care of, Sir.”

“See that you do, Mr. Contee and let me know when the woman is neutralized.”

Monday morning, Ralph was at the Department of Motor Vehicles in Cincinnati. His girlfriend, Elizabeth, worked there. “Beth Sweetheart, I need your help again.”

“Is this for a job?”

“No baby, I did a job Saturday night and I think some one got a good look at me.

“Saturday night, the Senator, was that you?”

“Yours truly, baby.”

All she could say was "WOW, what can I do to help?"

"I need to know who this license plate number belongs to."

In a few minutes she returned and told Ralph, "Marlo Huston, 1387 Anderson Road, Cincinnati. She's reporter for the City Examiner."

"Thanks Babe, I'll see you later tonight."

Chapter 23

"Come on Jack, you're scaring me."

"I'm not kidding Marlo. You have to be very careful. Don't open your door to anyone unless you know them, and only then if you can see them."

"Okay," she replied.

"Marlo, I got a hunch you might be able to help me with some research. I talked to a young lady a few days ago. She told me that a kid from my home town was supposed to take some training to be an assassin. She told me she thought another person involved was named Holton, or something like that. All I know is the training is supposed to be somewhere in south west Ohio. I imagine it would encompass a lot of land to set up a training course. Can you check the newspaper files to see if any large land sales have been recorded in the last year or so? Grady has to head back to Ironton, but I'm going to stick around a few days. There's something going on and I need some time to work on it".

"I can do that, Where can I get in touch with you?"

"I'll stay at the Park Lane for a night or two and then I'll find something less expensive."

She told us, "I'm going home. I'm tired and I do have to go to work in the morning."

"Marlo, before you go, Can you check on what kind of programs the Senator was working on?"

"Shoot, I can tell you that. He was working on a bill that advocates equality among the races. He was working on making the KKK and other supremacy groups illegal. You knew that Senator Hartly was Jewish, didn't you?"

"No I didn't, but that makes no difference."

Marlo arrived home around 1:15 PM Monday morning and after a few hours sleep, she headed for the newspaper office. She spent the next eight hours researching the files and around 7:00 PM, she headed back home. As the sun went down, she headed towards Anderson Road, a street of neat, white painted cottages. Lawns trimmed neatly and blue shutters gave the houses a spic and span look. She was concerned about what Jack told her; be careful. She had been trained in self defense and knew she would take care of herself if she saw it coming. What concerned her the most was the fight she couldn't see coming. The Senator never saw it coming and now he's dead. She knew she would have to be vigilante and look for things out of the ordinary.

Marlo pulled on to Anderson Road around 8:00 PM. The sun had set a little while ago and about a block from her house, she noticed a car parked in the street, a late model Lincoln. While the people in her neighborhood were not poor, they usually drove something less expensive; In fact,

Marlo drove a pick up truck. She continued on towards her house and the closer she got, the more apprehensive she became. Her father taught her to always pay attention to her gut feeling so she drove on past the house and parked a block away. Slipping out of her truck, she moved quietly under the cover of darkness towards her house. When she was a few doors from her house, she slipped between houses and continued along the alley. Quietly opening the gate, she glided through the back yard. Ralph Contee did not hear her sneaking up behind him. The forsythia bush gave him good cover from the front, but from the rear his ass was sticking out.

Marlo was within five feet of him and he never realized it. She screamed loudly and startled him. Ralph jumped up, started to turn around and about three quarters of the way around, Marlo hit him in the head with a round house kick.

"You bitch, I'm going to kill you," Ralph screamed.

"Maybe someday," Marlo replied, "but not tonight."

She delivered another round house kick to his head and the force of the kick caused Ralph to drop the gun. Being a former Special Forces service man, Ralph immediately pulled a knife from the sheath on his thigh and started at her.

The first lunge, Marlo deftly side stepped and delivered a bone crushing blow to his nose. The second lunge was Ralph's second mistake. Marlo ducked under the thrust and grabbed his hand, smashing it against the house, causing the knife to fall harmlessly to the ground. Now it was hand to hand. Ralph was throwing some real hay makers, most of which Marlo avoided by ducking and dodging. Ralph landed one hard blow to the side of her head and it stunned her for a few seconds. When she shook off the effects of the punch, she saw Ralph frantically searching for the pistol. She saw a glint of moonlight on the knife blade. Ralph wrapped his fingers around the pistol and fired, but Marlo was no longer there. Marlo had executed a body roll and came up with the knife. Throwing it with deadly aim, the knife hit Ralph in the right shoulder. He had enough and took off running, dropping the pistol as he held his shoulder. She thought about pursuing him, but decided not to push her luck.

She ran in the house and called the Park Lane Hotel. "Park lane Hotel, how may I help you?"

"Jack Steven's room please."

"Hello."

"Jack, this is Marlo. That guy that was at the hotel tried to kill me tonight. We kind of got in a fight and I kind of kicked his butt. He left here with a knife sticking out of his shoulder. He dropped his gun and I used a hanky to bring it in the house.

"Are you okay?"

"Yes, I'm okay."

"Did you call the police?"

"You are the police."

"You need to call the Cincinnati Police."

"I'll do that in a minute."

"Where do you live, Marlo?"

"1387 Anderson Road."

"I'll be there soon."

The hotel clerk gave me directions and I was sitting in front of Marlo's house in thirty minutes. The Cincinnati Police were already there. I jumped out of the car and showed them My ID. "I'm Jack Stevens, Federal Agent. There's been an attempted murder here and the intended victim, Marlo Huston, is inside with the pistol from the attacker. She kind of kicked his ass and managed to pick up the gun when he dropped it. I'd like for that weapon to be dusted for finger prints. I believe it's the same weapon that killed Senator Hartly and a police officer in Ironton. In the house, Marlo retrieved the pistol, a 45 with a silencer.

"Marlo, you didn't touch that pistol, did you?"

"No, I used a hanky to pick it up by the barrel."

"Great, give it to Officer Stanton, he's going to have it dusted for finger prints.

Marlo turned the pistol over to Officer Stanton and he said he would put out the word to the hospitals to be on the look out for a knife wound, right shoulder.

"That's a nasty looking bruise on the side of your face, Marlo."

"Yeah, he managed to get in one good punch, but a little make up will cover it."

"Tell me exactly what happened."

She proceeded to tell me the whole story from the time

she noticed the luxury car until he ran off.

After the police left, Marlo offered me a beer and we sat around and talked for a few minutes. All of a sudden, she started shaking violently, "Damn, I just realized I could have been killed tonight."

"But you weren't," I said. "I'm proud of you. You took on a killer and held your own. In fact, I'd say you kicked his ass, wouldn't you?"

"You're right; I did kick his ass, didn't I?"

"Miss Huston, I agree. I'm humbled in your presence."

"Now, you're making fun of me."

"No I'm not. I'm truly impressed by your actions tonight."

"What if he comes back?"

"I don't think he will want to cross blades with you again tonight."

"You don't think so?"

"No, why would he give you another chance to kick his ass again."

"You want another beer, Jack?"

"Sure, I'll have one more."

We sat on the couch and talked for a little while longer and I could tell she was still keyed up. I stood and walked around behind her and started massaging her shoulders. She leaned back and said, "That feels good." Continuing the massage, I started caressing her neck and lightly touching her ear lobes. My finger tips lightly caressed her throat and under her chin. Tracing her lips with my fingers caused a small, almost inaudible, sigh to escape from her lips. Gathering her hair to one side, I leaned down and kissed her neck. As I continued to kiss and caress her neck, the sighs became moans. Marlo turned and raised her lips to meet mine. As our lips were pressed together, I slid my hands down the front of her blouse and gently cupped her breasts. Suddenly, she broke away from the kiss and looked like she had tears in her eyes.

"What's the matter, Marlo?"

"I...I...can't do this."

"We don't have to," I replied. "I just felt there was an attraction between us."

"There is an attraction, Jack, but I have a boyfriend back home that I love very much."

"Oh," I said, "I'm sorry I saw something that wasn't there."

"It's there Jack, but I just can't cheat on him."

"I understand," I replied

"Marlo, it's getting late and I think you should get to bed. Are you going to be okay?"

"Yeah, I guess I'm a little tired."

"Listen, I've got an extra 38 in the car. I'll leave it if you want. Can you shoot?"

"Yeah, I have quite a bit of practice with a 38."

After we doubled checked all the doors and windows, I went to the car and retrieved the 38. Back at the door, I handed her the pistol. Just before she closed the door, I placed a kiss on my finger tips and lightly touched her cheek. “Make sure you lock this door. By the way, tell your boyfriend back home, he is a very lucky man.”

Reaching the Park Lane around midnight, I left a wake up call for 6:00 AM and hauled my tired butt to bed.

Chapter 24

Ralph made it back to his car and cleared the area before any cops showed up. He considered removing the knife from his shoulder but didn't know how much he would bleed. The bleeding had pretty much stopped by the time he got out of the city limits. The wound was hurting like hell, but he had been in more pain in Vietnam. In the fall of 61, he had been captured and tortured for two weeks before his unit overran the camp and rescued him. That experience turned Ralph into a vengeful person and he took it out on the Vietnamese people. He didn't care, north or south, they all looked the same to him. Because of his actions, Ralph spent a year in the brig and received a dishonorable discharge. After his separation form the Army, Ralph stayed in California for a few months. Hardly a day went by when he didn't pick a fight with an enlisted man; in fact Ralph spent many a day in the lock up for disorderly conduct. During one of the times he was out, he met Russ Holden. The last time Ralph was in the slammer, he called Russ to bail him out.

Around 2:00 AM, Ralph pulled up to the gate at the training camp and was allowed entrance by the sentry, a young kid about nineteen. With the knife still sticking in his shoulder, he knocked on the Captain's door. "Who is it?" The Captain asked.

"Ralph Contee, Sir."

"What do you want?"

"I'm reporting in from my mission, Sir."

"Hold on a minute."

When Captain Ron opened the door, the first thing he said was, "Mr. Contee, is that your knife sticking out of your shoulder?"

"Yes Sir."

"Why is it there and not in your sheath?"

"That woman reporter stuck it there, Sir"

"Is she dead?"

"No Sir."

"Mr. Contee, this is the second time you let her get away. Do you have an answer as to why?"

"No Sir."

The Captain snatched the knife from Ralph's shoulder and promptly drove it deep into Ralph's chest.

"Mr. Contee, I do not accept failure."

The Captain yelled for the sentry, "Come and get his dead ass and drag him over to the survival compound. Let the wolves eat him."

CHAPTER 25

I arose when the alarm went off at 6: AM. After a shower and dressing, I walked around the corner to Lou's Deli, devoured a couple of donuts and gulped down a cup of coffee. I used the pay phone in the deli to report to Dickerson and explain what went on last night. "I'll call later if the Cincinnati Police get a match on the finger prints. If not, I'll see that they send the prints to the FBI in Washington."

"Keep me posted Jack, this Senator Hartly thing has Congress breathing down our necks. We need to solve this one."

"We're on it Dickerson."

My first stop was the Cincinnati Police Department. Lt. John Imes told me they matched the print around 5:00 AM this morning.

"They belong to Ralph Contee, an ex Army Special Forces. He was held on a disorderly in a little town near Fort Ord. He had been in and out of trouble for a year or so. The last time he was in, about eight months ago, he was bailed out by a Russ Holden. Holden gave his address as 1079 Willow Street, here in Cincinnati. I don't know what the connection is between Holden and Contee; anyway, we sent a car out to Willow Street. Isn't any such number on Willow."

When I heard the name Holden, bells started ringing in my head.

"Imes, I had an informant tell me, several months ago, there was a training camp for assassins in south west Ohio. The informant also mentioned a name they thought was Holton. Holden is to close a match to be coincidence. Have you heard any scuttlebutt about an assassins training camp?"

"No, but I'll put the word out to our informants, see if we get a bite."

I left the police department and drove over to the City Examiner. Exiting the elevator on the second floor, I asked the receptionist where I could find Marlo Huston.

"You have to go down this hall, past four doors, turn left, and pass three more doors and... Wait, let me call her and tell her you're here. May I tell her who wants to see her?"

"Federal Agent Jack Stevens."

"Ooooooh, has she been a bad girl?"

"No Ma'am, I just need to talk to her."

She called Marlo and told her, "Marlo, Federal Agent Jack Stevens here to see you. Okay, I'll tell him you will be up in a couple of minutes."

A couple of minutes later Marlo came walking down the hall. She was wearing an olive green blouse and white slacks. She walked with an air of confidence, hips swaying side to side, and her thick red hair bouncing with every step she took. "Hello Jack," she said as she extended her hand, "How are you this morning?"

"WOW," I said as she ran her fingers through her hair, "You look great."

After getting over how good she looked, I noticed the bruise was hardly noticeable.

"Marlo, I have some information that may help you in your research. The guys name the other night was Ralph Contee. He's ex Special Forces and was in South East Asia until he received a dishonorable discharge for roughing up people. He was from the west coast and was bailed out of jail, on a disorderly, by a Russ Holden. Can you do some research on the two of them? Also, do you have any contacts on the west coast?"

"No, but I can go myself. I have some vacation and I can take a few days to do the research, stop off in Montana for a few days and be back in a week or so."

"Great, I'll be gone for a few days myself. I have to be at the trial for Robert Jenkins."

Chapter 26

Since Dr. Robert Jenkins crossed state lines in the commission of four of the murders and the fact that kidnapping charges were also filed against him, he was tried in Federal court. After a two week trial, he was found guilty on all nine counts of murder. Jenkins had the unfortunate luck of being in the court of The Hanging Judge, Roscoe Barnett. Judge Barnett was known far and wide for his no nonsense approach to his duties. I don't believe I would want to go before him for anything. Something as trivial as a parking ticket would make me shake in fear if he was the presiding Judge.

"Mr. Jenkins, you have been found guilty, by a jury of your peers, of nine counts of murder. You are to be held in custody by the US Marshall and detained at the Summit Correctional Facility until sentencing. Your sentence will be handed down two weeks from today.

The two weeks passed quickly. Doctor Robert Jenkins stood in front of Judge Barnett. "Mr. Jenkins, you are sentenced to die by electrocution on August 1st. 1964. May God have mercy on your soul."

After the sentence was handed down, I headed beck to

Cincinnati. The first order of business was to see what progress Imes had made on finding Contee and Holden.

"Jack, we've run up against a brick wall. Neither of the suspects can be found and we've searched half the state. It's like they disappeared into thin air. We got a couple of rumors about a training camp, but nobody knows where it is."

"Imes, I've got a contact that may be able to help us out. I'll let you know if I find out anything."

I left the police department and drove over to the Examiner. The receptionist called Marlo, "Marlo that agent is back."

"Tell him to start down the hall, I'll meet him."

I started down the hall and turned left after the fourth door before I saw her coming towards me. "Hi Marlo. How are you?"

"Great and how are you?"

"Great also, when did you get back?"

"I got back a couple of days ago. I took a couple of extra days in Montana to visit family and my ex boyfriend."

"What do you mean, ex?"

"He thought I was coming home to settle down and have babies with him. I told him my job was important to me and I wasn't ready to have babies because I wanted to spend five more years being a reporter. I asked him to come to Ohio. He's an electrician and he can get a job anywhere. He told me he wasn't coming to Ohio and it was the job or him. I told him I loved him but I wasn't giving up my job for him or any other man. So, here I am."

"You okay?' I asked.

"Yes, I'm fine. It's his loss. Come on back to my office, have I got a story for you."

We walked down the hall to her office, a corner office with two windows. One view was a brick wall and the other was a view of the alley behind the Examiner.

"Russ Holden was originally from LA. His Mother and Father were real estate investors in LA. About four years ago, they were killed in a car wreck and left their entire estate to Russ, his brother Ron and a sister, Rose. The estate was valued at a little over three million. The three siblings liquidated the estate and walked away with over two million cash. Word is they bought a five hundred acre farm outside Cincinnati about three years ago. Contee was a dishonorable discharge from Special Forces and Russ Holden bailed him out of LA jail about nine months ago."

"Good work, Marlo. You're an impressive young lady. I'm sure you'll go far. Were you able to determine where they bought?"

"Not yet, but I'm searching the real estate records starting back four years ago. I'll let you know when I find it."

Back at the hotel, I had nothing to do but wait. Tuesday evening Marlo called,

"Jack, I found it. A five hundred acre farm sold in Bainbridge, Ohio. I got the address. Are you going to go out and bust them?"

"Not yet, I have to make sure it's the right place."

"When you going?" she asked.

"Wednesday morning."

"Can I come along?"

"I don't know Marlo. You know it could be dangerous."

"I know that. Besides, you know I can take care of myself. On top of that, I know the road. You'd have to hunt all over the county to find it."

"I don't like it but you kind of have me over a barrel. I'll pick you up around 8:00 AM. We'll do a slow drive by to see if we can spot anything unusual. We'll have to be very careful as they may be sentries posted."

Wednesday morning, I picked up Marlo and two hours later we were driving down Lyons Creek Road.

"We should be getting close," she said.

About a mile farther, we passed a gate that was newer than the fence it was attached to it.

"Stop," she said. "I bet this is it."

"I can't stop here. What if there is a sentry just inside that wood line. We'd be sitting ducks. I don't know about you, but I don't have a death wish. We'll drive on by and come back tonight. I prefer to do my snooping under the cover of darkness. I don't think they know we're close and I'd like it to stay that way. I need to get back to a pay phone."

Chapter 27

"Dickerson, this is Jack. I think we have a good lead in Don's and the Senator's cases and I need a couple of things. One, I need a chopper to make a flyover outside Bainbridge, Ohio. The area I need is twelve miles north of Bainbridge and four miles west. We can only make one pass because I don't want to alert them. There's a big open field ten miles south of Bainbridge where the chopper can set down. I can meet them there and give explicit instructions and directions to the area. Can you get it done?"

"Yeah, I think so. It will probably be tomorrow as the weather at the airfield is kind of nasty right now. Call me back around 5:00 o'clock to be sure for tomorrow. What was the second thing?"

"Do the Feds have anything to help see in the dark? I'd heard some stories but I didn't know if they were true."

"It's something kind of experimental right now. They pick up movement and use infrared to pick up body heat."

"That's all I need right now. Can you send two?"

"Why do you need them?"

"I need to get close to the place at night so I can see how it is laid out."

"Who's the other set for?"

"I got a helper."

"Well, tell him to be careful, those damn things cost big bucks."

"Okay, I tell him. I'll talk to you a 5:00 o'clock."

I didn't dare tell him they were for a female civilian.

Five PM rolled around and I was back on the phone with Dickerson.

"Jack, be at the Cincinnati Airport at 9:00 AM tomorrow. I got a chopper to pick you up there. He'll do a fly over with you."

"What do you mean, with me?"

"Jack, you have to direct him where you want to go. You're not afraid to fly, are you?"

"No, it's just that I've never been in a helicopter before."

"Well, like it or not, be there a 9:00 AM, gate three. By the way, it's a two seater and your friend will have to stay on the ground."

I hung up the phone and asked Marlo if she was hungry.

"Yeah," she replied.

After getting a bite to eat at a truck stop on US 52, I took Marlo home. I went in with her to make sure the house was secure. Just as I started towards the front door to leave, Marlo walked towards me, tilted her head up and kissed me. Her lips were warm and inviting as I returned the kiss. After out lips parted, I asked her, "Marlo, do you know what you're doing?"

"Yes," she replied, "I want you to make love to me."

"Marlo, I would very like very much to make love to you but I don't think you're quite ready for that. You're not over your boy friend yet and I don't think your love dies that easy. It's only been a few days." We stood there in an embrace and as I looked into her eyes, I could see the tears start to well up in the corner of her eyes. She still loved him and I knew it.

"Thank you, Jack. You're right, I'm not over him."

When I walked to the door, I stopped, placed a kiss on my finger tips and reached out and touched her lips. "I'll pick you up around 6:00 PM tomorrow. We'll go out and see what's going on at the camp, okay?"

"I thought I would go on the helicopter with you tomorrow morning."

"Sorry, it's a two seater, just me and the pilot."

"Oh well, I tried," she said.

I'm at gate three at the appointed time. A small helicopter sets down about fifty yards away. Markings on the tail showed the number, along with the name, Huron Oil. The pilot stepped out and started walking to gate three.

"Are you Jack Stevens?"

"Yes."

"Come on, we're going for a ride."

I got in and hooked the belt as he went through the checklist of re-starting the engine.

"Why is an oil company providing a chopper?" I asked. "I thought the State Police had one."

"This is a State Police unit. We have several signs we can switch on the tail. You don't want to do surveillance with this bird marked Ohio State Police, do you?"

"You got a point. Are you familiar with Bainbridge, Ohio?"

"Yes."

"Good. That's where we're headed."

The pilot said everyone called him Stoney. Stoney and I lifted off and in a short while we were approaching Bainbridge. "Go north about twelve miles and then head west. When we get to a big pond on the right hand side of the road, that's Lyons Creek Road. We'll head west there." About two miles down Lyons Creek, I asked him to start veering right. "Go slow enough and low enough so I can see, but not so low to arouse suspicion if we cross over the camp." After a few minutes, we noticed a clearing up ahead. As we entered the east side of the clearing, I noticed five men run out of the woods, carrying weapons. "Stoney, keep it steady and straight ahead."

The sentries reported to Captain Ron Holden, "Sir, a helicopter just flew over."

"How low was it?"

"It was about five hundred feet Sir."

"Were there any markings on it?"

"Recruit Donaldson put the glasses on it. He said it was marked Huron Oil, Sir."

"It was probably flying some executive to a meeting, but just in case, double the watch tonight."

"Yes Sir."

Stoney kept it in a straight line past the camp clearing. About a hundred and fifty yards past the main clearing, I couldn't believe my eyes. A pack of wolves were fighting over what appeared to be a human carcass.

"Stoney, look down to your right. Tell me what you see."

"Looks like a pack of wolves, to me."

"Maybe I'm crazy," I said, "but I'd swear that looks like a man's body."

We flew in a straight line for another ten minutes and then veered left towards the Cincinnati Airport. By noon, I was back in the police station talking to Captain Imes. I told him of my plans to scout the camp tonight.

"Be careful, Jack, you never know what kind of traps they may have."

After picking up Marlo, we headed for Bainbridge and arrived around 9:00 PM. We parked the car about a mile from the gate and started walking towards the camp. Within a half mile of the gate, we climbed over the fence and struck out in the direction of the main camp. "Okay Marlo, here's the deal. You do exactly as I ask. These guys are armed to the teeth and I want both of us to come out of here alive, okay?'

'Okay," she replied nervously.

"You sure you want to do this?"

"Yeah, I'm sure."

We started off at a very slow pace. Every twenty feet or so, I'd stop and slip the goggles up to my eyes.

"What are we looking for?' she asked.

"I'm looking for anything that moves, no matter how slight. These goggles will detect body heat from any living creature. It will show up red in the goggles. From now on, when I put the goggles on, I want you to put yours on." We moved about two hundred yards when Marlo whispered,

"I see something."

"Where?" I asked.

"Straight ahead and a little to the left." she said

I looked in that direction and I also saw the image. It was too big to be an animal. Suddenly it arose and walked about ten feet, stepped over something and continued to walk another twenty feet. I thought he spotted us until he stopped and it looked like he unzipped his pants. Sure enough, a red stream was spewing from his groin area. Walking back, he stepped across and resumed his post.

I whispered to Marlo, "That thing he stepped across has got to be a booby trap. We need to take him out so we can get closer to the camp. We're going to sneak up to within thirty feet of him. You stay put, while I get a little closer. After you get set, give me ten minutes to get a little closer and then you start breaking some twigs. When he comes to investigate, I'll whack him." About two minutes after I was set, I heard the twigs breaking. I saw him tense up and stand. Cautiously stepping over the booby trap, he was not expecting me. I hit him in the throat and he dropped his weapon and stumbled backwards. All of a sudden, I heard a swoosh. He evidently tripped the wire as a big eight by eight foot board came swinging down from a tree. When it stopped swinging, he was impaled on sharpened wood sticks.

Marlo came walking up and was thoroughly grossed out by the sight of all the sticks protruding from his body. By midnight, we were close enough to see the compound. With six small buildings, there couldn't be a whole lot of people there. Maybe twenty or thirty tops. We were very careful to exit the camp the same way we came in. By 6:00 AM we were back at Marlo's house and she was fixing us breakfast. She was as good a cook as she was good looking. She went to bed for a few hours and I went to the Cincinnati Police. After filling them in on everything, we made plans to raid the camp at 5:00 AM the next morning.

The State Police, Federal Agents and the Cincinnati Police came charging through the compound gate. The raid was a complete success. Three of the Captain's recruits were killed, as well as Captain Ron Holden. Russ and Rose surrendered, along with eighteen recruits. I told Captain Imes, "I have to go back in the woods about hundred and fifty yards. There's another clearing and I think there's a body back there. I took a couple of officers with me and we made it to the clearing in fifteen minutes. In the clearing, lay a partial skeleton. The skull and the rib cage were easily recognizable. We looked around and found bits and pieces of clothing. Anderson, one of the officers said, “Jack, over here.”

“What you got?”

“It’s a piece of camo outfit, looks like it has a pocket still attached.”

I walked over and picked it up and there was something in the pocket. I reached in and pulled out a wallet. After opening the wallet, I found an ID for Ralph Contee. Retribution wasn’t swift but it certainly was terrible

I drove back to Cincinnati and arrived at Marlo’s house around 3:00 PM. “Marlo, you can write your story.”

“What happened at the camp?”

I took the next two hours and told her what happened. As I was getting ready to leave, she told me,

“My boyfriend called yesterday, he’s moving to Ohio and we’re getting back together.”

That’s great,” I said, “He’s a lucky man.”

Around 5:30, I started back to Ironton. All the way back, I kept wondering, What if.

The Final Chapter

Doctor Robert Jenkins was transferred from death row to the holding cell on July 1st, 1964. This would be his home until he kept his date with the executioner. That move, under tight security, was the beginning of his last thirty one days on earth. Barring intervention by the Governor or the Supreme Court, he would be put to death on August 1st. All the legal wrangling of his lawyer was fruitless. As the day grew closer, Jenkins gave up all hope of a reprieve and accepted the fact that the end of his life was near.

July 31st. Jenkins received his last meal at 6:00 PM. He looked at it for a while but he just could not force himself to take the first bite. As darkness closed in on the prison, three guards were going through the procedures for the electrocution. All the belts and electrical connections were checked and double checked. Several people would be witnessing this execution. Nine witnesses had been invited and six had responded, Widows Jennings and Hannon, Evelyn Waugh—Jane Ulster's Mother, Ed Hopkins Widow, Tom Castle's seventy year old Mother, and the Fire Chief of Catlettsburg would be in attendance.

I would be there for John Doe, Uncle Charlie, and Raymond Strong.

9:00 PM. Anti death penalty advocates were picketing on the sidewalk in front of the prison. When I pulled up to the main gate on the beast, a long haired freak came running towards me and yelled, "You're the one that put Jenkins in there to die."

About ten other pro lifers followed his example and started screaming at me. The crowd became deathly quiet when I stopped and shut off the beast. I got off and walked up to the long haired freak and grabbed his shirt. "Listen asshole, you're trying to save a man that killed nine people, plus he killed his own Mother. Do you want to know why he killed them?"

"Why?" he replied meekly

"Because he thought they were inferior and he enjoyed it. One of them was a patient of his since she was a young girl. Most of the others, he picked at random. Jenkins thought he was God and he alone could decide who lived and who died. You look different. What if he saw you out one night, would you have been his next victim? How would you feel with those huge powerful hands wrapped around your throat, crushing your windpipe? Would you be begging for your life, all the while trying to breathe and not being able to draw a breath? Can you honestly look in the eyes of the relatives of his victims and tell them he deserves to live?"

The long haired one just stood there and wouldn't even

look me in the eyes. I got back on the beast and rode through the main gate. In the office, a guard told me the witness room would open at 11.00 PM.

Over the next hour and a half, three people showed up. Mr. Watson, Tom Castle's Mother, and the Fire Chief of Catlettsburg, Kentucky. We acknowledged one another, but other than that, the conversation was minimal.

11:45 PM, Robert Jenkins received a visit from the Prison Chaplain. After the Chaplain left, three guards shackled Evans, hand and foot. At 11:50 PM, Evans was removed from his cell and walked the last few steps of his life. In the death chamber, he was strapped in the chair; a metal skull cap was placed over his head followed by a black hood.

12:00 midnight. The curtains in the witness room were opened. The assistant warden read the charges against him and reiterated the death sentence.

12:02 PM August 1st. The death sentence was carried out. When the electric hit Jenkins, his body jerked violently and tendrils of smoke rolled out from under the hood. Another surge of electricity caused him to jerk violently again and then his body slumped in the chair. A few minutes later, the prison doctor pronounced him dead. The time was 12:10 AM, August 1st. 1964. Two guards entered the chamber and started removing the straps. As the guard removed the strap from his left arm, his hand relaxed. His fingers uncurled and two nickels fell to the floor. Jenkins just used a little traveling money for his trip to hell.

After the execution of Dr. Robert Jenkins, I straddled the beast and rode off in the moonlight. As I traveled the back roads of Kentucky, I wondered what would be my next assignment.